PROTECTING CLOVER (SPECIAL FORCES: OPERATION ALPHA)

SEARCH & RESCUE BOOK 2

JEN TALTY

To the love of my life! You rock my world.

Dear Readers,

Welcome to the Special Forces: Operation Alpha Fan-Fiction world!

If you are new to this amazing world, in a nutshell the author wrote a story using one or more of my characters in it. Sometimes that character has a major role in the story, and other times they are only mentioned briefly. This is perfectly legal and allowable because they are going through Aces Press to publish the story.

This book is entirely the work of the author who wrote it. While I might have assisted with brainstorming and other ideas about which of my characters to use, I didn't have any part in the process or writing or editing the story.

I'm proud and excited that so many authors loved my characters enough that they wanted to write them into their own story. Thank you for supporting them, and me!

READ ON!

Xoxo

Susan Stoker

CHAPTER 1

Clover Sullivan set her guitar in the stand and stepped from the stage. Pride filled her heart as she looked out over the dining room of the Sans. A few people sat at the bar, and there were three full tables left over from the lunch crowd. They had turned their attention away from her and back to their meals and conversations. Playing a set in the middle of the day always settled her nervous energy. She glanced at her watch. Wyatt should be done with debriefing by the time the dinner patrons rolled in. She scurried across the room and snagged the reserved sign and placed it on the big table in the middle of the room. Keeping the Sans after her father had died had been the best decision she'd ever made. It gave her a place to sing and write, with an income that afforded her to follow her passion.

It also gave Wyatt a place to land where she could be a constant part of his life.

Her pulse went into high gear. Having Wyatt living in the same town stirred so many emotions. In some ways he brought her comfort and made her feel closer to her father's memory.

But it also made her feel like a crazy teenager with her first crush.

She smiled. Wyatt had been her first crush, and her feelings for him had continued to grow over the years, but between the age difference and his marriage, then divorce, she'd never really had a chance to make a move.

That would change tonight.

Right after he had a chance to digest the news she'd found out about his ex-wife.

"What has you smiling?" Chris Miller, the Sans Bar and Grill manager asked. He set a package on the table. "Oh. He comes back tonight."

"What's your problem with Wyatt?" she asked, wishing she hadn't sounded so annoyed. Chris had been a good friend over the years, and he deserved her respect.

"I don't have a problem with him, but I don't

understand why you're pining for a man who doesn't even notice you exist." Chris tapped his long fingers over the box.

"Wyatt and I go way back. It's not like that with him." Of course, Wyatt hadn't noticed her because she hadn't given him a reason to. When he'd gotten divorced, she had gotten engaged to Reagan, the one and only SEAL she'd ever had a relationship with and one of the reasons she had decided to never date another one again.

However, she could no longer deny her feelings for Wyatt, and it was high time he knew she cared about him, and not just as a friend.

"You deserve someone who will appreciate you and spoil you, not treat you like an afterthought," Chris said.

Wyatt might not be the most attentive man, but he certainly didn't treat her poorly. He just kept everyone at a safe distance, and for good reasons. Besides, Chris was still bitter over the fact she and he didn't hit it off.

At all.

And it only took two dates for her to figure that out, but he still hadn't accepted it.

New rule: Never date co-workers, especially employees. Chris was the best manager the Sans has had in a long while, and she didn't want to lose him.

She curled her fingers around his biceps. "Thank you for looking out for me. But, for the record, I don't date SEALs. You know that. Wyatt and I are just friends." For now, but she wasn't about to confide in Chris, or anyone for that matter.

If she crashed and burned, no one needed to watch.

"I care about you." Chris inched closer.

She moved back.

He frowned. "We would be good together."

"Chris. I'm sorry. I really am, but we're better off as friends. I can't do a relationship right now with anyone."

"Because you're hung up on him," he muttered. "One of these days you're going to see that he's no good for you, and I am, but I'm not going to wait around forever."

"I thought you were dating that cute redhead that comes in every once in a while."

"We're friends, and I've thought about it," he said.

"You should go for it, because you and me as a couple isn't going to happen. Your friendship is important to me, and I hope we can find a way to migrate back to that type of relationship."

"I have to value your honesty." He nodded, giving her a little smile. "Before I forget, this package was delivered for you during your set."

She lifted the box. No return address and it hadn't been mailed since it only had her name written on it in big bold black letters. "Who dropped it off?"

"Delivery girl of some kind. I assume a private courier. She had me sign for it."

"I'm not expecting anything." Maybe Wyatt sent her a gift from his latest deployment. It wouldn't be the first time he'd done something sweet like that. With excitement bubbling across her skin, she took a knife and ripped open the tape. Flipping open the flaps, she peeked inside.

"Oh, my God." She tossed the box to the table and brought her trembling hands to her face, muting her scream.

Chris tipped the package, dumping out a dismembered Barbie doll with a broken tiny play guitar. "Shit." He wrapped his arms around her and tucked her head to his chest. "I'll call the police."

"Who would do such a thing?"

"A sick bastard who has it in for you. I could name at least three weirdos that come in here just to drool over you while you sing."

She stepped from Chris' overly protective embrace and plucked her cell from her back pocket. Snapping a picture of the doll, she sent it to Keanu.

Clover: This came just now. Calling the cops. DON'T tell Wyatt. I'll talk to him tonight about it. And DON'T worry and come rushing over. Cops are on the way. See you tonight.

Keanu had been one of her father's best friends. He'd also been the last one to see her father alive. He all but died in Keanu's arms.

Keanu: I'll call my cop buddy Dave. Who are you with?

Clover: Chris is here. Dinner staff is arriving soon.

Keanu: Make sure they do a sweep of the bar. Hang tight. Don't go anywhere alone. Got it?

Clover: Loud and clear.

"The police are on the way," Chris said. "I wish I could remember the name of the courier."

"What about the hostess?" Clover inspected everyone in the restaurant. A couple of locals sat at the bar, and two families occupied a couple of tables.

"I let her go early." Chris looped his arm over her shoulder. "Come on. Let's sit down over there." He pointed to a high-top near the front of the bar. "We'll be able to see when the cops roll in."

Her heart pounded against her throat, making it difficult to swallow. "Was there a note or anything?"

"Didn't appear to be," Chris said, pushing a glass of water in front of her. "Would like me to go look?"

"Do you mind?"

"Not at all." He patted her shoulder. "Drink that, okay?"

She raised the glass to her lips and swallowed a few gulps. The cold water trickled down her throat, slamming into her stomach.

"No note," Chris said. "Can I get you anything else?"

"I'm okay, thanks." For the next ten minutes, she sipped the cool liquid and stared out the window, trying not to glance over at the doll with missing limbs. Why would anyone send her a doll? Even if the Barbie had all its limbs still attached, it was an odd gift.

The door swished open, and two police officers strolled in with their hands looped into their belts. A plain clothes cop followed a couple of steps behind.

She recognized him as Dave Watson, a good friend of Keanu's as well as Wyatt. If memory served her correctly, Dave spent six years in the Navy and had gone through bootcamp with Keanu.

"It's good to see you again, but not under these

circumstances," Dave said as he made his way to the broken doll. "Who accepted the package?"

"I did," Chris said, extending his hand. "A young lady, maybe twenty, with shoulder-length blond hair and blue eyes, I think, dropped it off. She wore black slacks and a red shirt that I thought had some kind of logo on it."

"I didn't ask for all those details." Dave arched a brow as he glanced between Chris and the doll. "But they will come in handy. Anything else you want to tell me?"

Chris opened his mouth but then snapped it shut, looking all indignant.

Clover want to interject, asking Dave to give Chris a break, that he was just trying to be helpful, but that would spur Chris on to be more overbearing and protective, and that was the last thing Clover wanted.

"What did this girl say?" Dave asked as he took pictures of the doll and all its broken pieces.

"Just that she had a package for Clover, and she made me sign for it on a tablet of some kind," Chris said.

"Do you normally get packages at work?" Dave asked as he snapped on gloves and studied the box.

One of the officers stood by the door, not allowing anyone in or out.

"We get all sorts of deliveries," Chris said.

"That question was directed at Clover." Dave pointed to the other police officer who held up a plastic bag.

"I've been known to order things and have them shipped here, and friends have sent me things to the bar before." She stood next to Chris with her arms folded across her chest. A cool shiver prickled her spine.

"Does the doll represent or mean anything special to you?" After Dave put everything in plastic evidence bags, he handed it to the police officer.

"I used to play with Barbies when I was a kid, but that's about it." Clover shook her head. "Why would someone send me a broken doll with a smashed tiny toy guitar?"

"What kind of enemies do you have? Ex-boyfriends with an axe to grind. Or past employees. Jealous people in the industry."

She pinched the bridge of her nose. "I had to fire a waitress last week for stealing, but other than that, I can't think of anyone. I pretty much keep to myself and do my thing."

. . .

"We'll check out the waitress. Can you make me a list of anyone who you might have pissed off or who has reason to want to scare or hurt you?"

"It will be a short list."

"Take a little time and think about it. Even the smallest of fights could have huge consequences. So, even if you believe someone would never do something like this, but you had a disagreement with them of any kind, I want them on that list, okay?"

"Okay," she said softly.

"Do you mind if we interview everyone in the bar before we leave?" Dave asked.

"I'd rather you not—"

She interrupted Chris. "Do what you need to, just please explain to my customers they have nothing to worry about."

"We'll let you know what we find out. In the meantime, be on the lookout, and if anything else happens, call 9-1-1 and have them call me." He handed her a business card.

"Thank you," she said.

"My pleasure. Say hello to Keanu and Wyatt for me."

"They will be here a little later," she said.

"Good." Dave shoved his hands into his trousers and headed toward the bar.

"That's it? That's all he's going to do?" The words tumbled out of Chris' mouth as more of a statement and not a question. "He's not taking this seriously at all. They should be putting a protection detail on you or something." Chris shook his head. "Maybe you should stay with me until this is over."

She bit down on her tongue to keep from laughing. "That's over the top. I'll be fine." She took a step toward her office.

Chris grabbed her arm. "Clover, someone threatened you, and I'm not about to let anything happen to you. So, if you're not going to stay with me, I'll camp out at your house."

"You will do no such thing," she said firmly. If she were to ask anyone for that kind of protection, it would be a trained professional. "I appreciate that you care, but I'm a big girl, and I will make sure I'm safe. I need you to do your job and run my restaurant, and if that courier comes back, let me and the cops know. Just keep an eye out here, okay?"

Chris squeezed her forearm with a gentle, kind touch. "I can do that but promise me you won't blow this off."

"Trust me, I won't," she said. "Now, I've got some work to do in my office."

No sooner did she get settled at her desk behind her laptop than her phone buzzed.

Wyatt: Keanu told me what happened, and I'm going to assume you walked to work. Consider me your personal bodyguard for the evening.

Her thumbs hovered over the screen. A warmth spread over her skin like a melting marshmallow, all gooey and sweet.

Don't do it.

Oh, bloody hell. What did she have to lose?

Clover: My body would love to be guarded by you... and maybe something else...

The little bubble appeared, indicating the promise of a response.

It disappeared and reappeared five times before her phone buzzed with a response.

Wyatt: Are you flirting with me?

She laughed. Damn straight she was.

Clover: See you when you get here. My body is waiting.

Wyatt: My guarding is coming.

Wyatt: That came out the wrong way. See you soon.

CHAPTER 2

The smell of burnt popcorn and fresh beer assaulted Navy SEAL Wyatt Johnson's nose the second he stepped into the Sans Bar and Grill, reminding him that there was no place like home, especially after a month-long training deployment.

But it was the sweet music of Clover Sullivan that soothed his aching soul. Her voice glided across his ears like hot syrup mixing with butter on a fluffy stack of pancakes. She sat up on the small stage and graced everyone with her vocal presence. She'd grown into a beautiful and strong woman, but Wyatt always knew she would, no matter what the world tossed in her direction. She had an old soul, a free spirit, and a heart made of gold.

"Every time I see her, it brings it all back," his task

commander, Lt. Keanu Kalen, said as he took a seat at a table reserved for the rest of the eight-man squad. Keanu, like every other SEAL Wyatt knew, had his own baggage he carried around like a badge of honor.

"Her father was a good man." Wyatt had first met Clover when she was in middle school when he served with her father, Colorado. She'd been a starry-eyed twelve-year-old, and Wyatt had been a twenty-two-year-old young man with an ego the size of Texas. He'd walked onto Colorado's team with a chip on his shoulder, but Colorado soon put him in his place. He had taught Wyatt humility, honor, and had been there with Wyatt when his precious baby boy had died eight years ago and the subsequent shitshow that happened shortly after with his ex-wife.

So had Clover.

In many ways, Wyatt owed his life to Colorado and Clover.

"The best," Keanu said solemnly as he waved to the waitress, holding up two fingers. "I wish I could go back and—"

"Don't go there." Wyatt understood that Keanu still held himself responsible for his previous team's death, but it was the furthest thing from the truth.

"And you better keep that shit in check around Clover. She sure as hell doesn't blame you, or your wife, for what happened."

"Look at you taking your task commander to task." Keanu held up his beer. "Have you talked to her since the Barbie doll incident?"

"I sent her a text, and she responded in usual fashion by letting me know she's a grown-ass woman, and the cops are handling it." Not to mention the flirting, but Wyatt wasn't going to bring that up with Keanu, for a plethora of reasons. One of them being he didn't want to have to listen to Keanu go on and on about how he and Clover would be a good fit.

Of course, Wyatt had to assume Clover was being sarcastic, or something. It would be best if he didn't read anything into the text messages.

Keanu nodded. "Dave is doing what he can to push forensics along, but he's got nothing. The waitress Clover fired was at her new job, but he's keeping an eye on her."

"What about the courier company?" Wyatt asked.

"Based on the description of the uniform, Dave thought it was Jensen Deliveries, only they have no record of a package being sent here." Keanu raised his hand. "And he's looked into all the other ones.

Nothing. Whoever sent the package doesn't want to be found, and that makes me insanely nervous."

Wyatt snapped his gaze back to the stage. Clover strummed her guitar. Her fingers glided over the strings like a master pianist. "I live two doors down, so I'll keep an eye on her."

"She's like a daughter to me, so I'm counting on you for exactly that. I know she's scared, but she's acting like it's just a stupid prank by an idiot who is jealous of her latest hits. Did she tell you about the song she sold to that big country band?"

"She sent me an email as soon as it happened. I didn't get it until the training session was over, but I'm thrilled for her, and I have a little surprise for her when she gets home." Wyatt smiled proudly.

"Home? Is there something you want to tell me?"

Wyatt groaned. "No." Damn. He should have known this conversation would lead to a discussion about his love life.

"Now tell me again why you and Clover aren't an item, because you act like a man in love half the time."

Wyatt shook his head and chose to ignore the question. He raised the longneck to his lips and sipped while he stared at Clover. Her lips moved over the mic as the sound system carried her magical voice into the room. When her gaze locked with his, she smiled, giving him a little nod. "Why didn't Ainsley come out with us tonight?" Wyatt asked, needing to change the focus.

"Not going to answer me, eh?" Keanu asked with a slight chuckle. "To answer yours, Karl has an ear infection, and he doesn't do well with a babysitter when he's like that. As a matter of fact, I'm under strict orders that I can only have one beer with the team, and then straight home."

"Why don't you go now?" Wyatt would give everything he had to be able to hug his son again. Not a day went by that he didn't think about Michael. He would have turned ten a couple of months ago. Wyatt wondered if he would have liked sports, or if he would have been more like his mother and a been a bookworm.

"I'm going to have my one beer and say hello to Clover," Keanu said. "For a new, young team, you all seemed to gel quite well together. I was pleased with the outcome of the training mission."

It was strange for Wyatt to be the oldest on any team. On his last squad, he'd been the baby, but after Operation Princess failed, and Colorado died, things changed. "Parker struggled a little with confidence but was fresh out of SEAL training when you formed this squad. The good news is he's smarter than fuck, and when it mattered, he didn't question his instincts. I'm happy with this squad, and we work well with the rest of the platoon."

"Good to know," Keanu said.

The crowd clapped and whistled as Clover's song ended.

"Thank you," Clover said. "I'm going to take a short break, but I'll be back with some new material." She set her guitar on a stand next to the stool. Her dark wavy hair flowed over her shoulders and down her back like a cascading waterfall.

Wyatt stood, setting his beer on the table. Living in Virginia again had both good memories and tragic ones. He did his best to hold on to the ones that gave him strength to get through the night. He stretched his arms out, and Clover ran right into them. Her hair smelled like coconut and vanilla. He resisted the urge to fist her hair and tug so that he could ravish her mouth with a hot, wet kiss that was meant for a private setting.

"Welcome home, sailor," she whispered in his ear right before her lips smacked his cheek. "I missed you."

"I missed you too." He held on a little longer than what most would deem appropriate for old friends.

Her body molded against his as if she were his favorite shirt. Everything about Clover awakened Wyatt, but he couldn't ever act on them.

"Hey, old man." She took a step back and embraced Keanu. "You must be happy to have your squad back in one piece."

"You know I am." He downed the rest of his brew before slamming it on the table. "I'm going to leave you two so you can catch up."

"Don't you want to be here when the rest of the gang gets here?" Wyatt asked, like a scared little boy being left alone for the very first time.

"Nah. I saw all you goons during debriefing. Enjoy your vacation time. I'll talk to you soon," Keanu said. "Clover, watch your back and lay low. Promise me you'll call Dave if anything is wonky and no walking back and forth to work alone."

She nodded. "I'm not stupid."

"Just stubborn," Wyatt muttered.

She nudged him in the gut with her elbow.

He laughed as he eased back into the booth and stared into Clover's chocolate-colored eyes. She'd been through a lot in her childhood, but she never let any of it dull the life that danced in those dark orbs.

"How are you holding up? This afternoon had to

have been frightening." Wyatt sipped his beverage, keeping his gaze on her face.

"I'd be lying if I told you it didn't freak me out, but even Dave said, without a note, we have no idea if the sender means to harm me or just scare the shit out of me, or even if it was supposed to be sent that way. It's possible the damage happened during delivery."

He scanned the room, making note of everyone in it. Two burly men at the bar stuck out. One glanced over his shoulder but quickly turned his attention back to his beer. "Let's hope the latter." He nodded to Chris who hovered over the hostess at the front door. "I hate to admit this, but I'm glad Chris was here."

"Me too." She smiled. "It's good to see you. I really missed you."

"It's good to be seen, but I'm exhausted and can't wait to sleep in my own bed." Every team or squad he'd been on had pre and post op traditions, but anytime he'd been stationed in Virginia, which had been most of his career as a SEAL, coming to the Sans had been more than a ritual. In some ways, it allowed him to pay homage to his long-time friend, Colorado, as well Wyatt's son.

She reached out and cupped his cheek. "You look

tired. Was it a hard mission? I try not to pay attention to anything military related on the news when you're deployed."

"It was just a training exercise." His smile faded. She'd been like that with her father too, only it hadn't kept him from being killed in the line of duty. What hurt the most about Colorado's death had been the fact that Kip, a mutual friend and fellow SEAL, had turned on his country and his fellow sailor.

And for what?

That was an answer that died with Kip.

She cocked her head. "I expect Keanu to give me that look, not you."

"Sorry." He pushed all the negative thoughts from his mind and focused on the pretty girl sitting across from him. "I did get your last message. Congratulations on the sale of two new songs. I wanted to respond, but once we boarded the transport plane, I was cut off from the rest of the world."

"I, of all people, understand." She leaned forward, taking his hands. "How long are you home for?"

"I've got the next five days off. After that, who knows. My team is ready, so we could be deployed anywhere at any time at this point."

"How does it feel to be the old man in charge?"

she asked with a tilt of her head and a sweet smile that sucker punched him right in the chest, sending his heart pounding into his throat.

"Weird. There are four men younger than you and about as green as I was when I first met your dad."

"My father loved you like a son. I remember after your first deployment on my dad's team, I told him I was going to marry you one day. He never laughed so hard in his life. I think he enjoyed telling me you were engaged."

"I got married a few months after that deployment," he said, swallowing hard. He and Gwen had truly loved one another, but the loss of a child, and the long separation of military life, took its toll, and Gwen couldn't handle it. "Your father hated every crush you had on his men, especially Keanu." Wyatt tapped his chest. "I was hurt over that one because he's even older than me."

She laughed. "My crush days are long gone."

He arched a brow as he held her hands a little tighter. "Really? So, does that mean you've found yourself a boyfriend? Or maybe you finally caved and went out with Chris?"

She rolled her eyes. "First, Chris isn't my type, and I think he's over me anyway. This redhead has been hanging around him lately, and he's enjoying the attention. And secondly, the only single men in this town are either military, or single for a reason."

"And you don't date military men," he said, letting out a long breath. One of the many reasons he'd always keep his feelings to himself. "Which I don't blame you. We're arrogant, and we're never home."

Tears welled in her eyes.

"What's wrong?" He leaned closer, bringing her hand to his lips. He kissed her warm skin. "Why are you about to cry? You know I don't handle crying women well."

"I hate to bring this up, but you're going to find out sooner or later, and I don't want it to be randomly where it will catch you off guard."

He swallowed. "What's going on?

"You know Gwen got married a few years ago."

Not only had he known, but his ex-wife thought it had been a good idea to invite him. Of course, he didn't attend, and that wasn't because he was bitter.

But he'd be lying if he didn't admit that stung that she could start over with someone else instead of working to save their marriage. Once their son passed, she'd checked herself out and never looked back. He, on the other hand, crawled under a rock and waited to die. Well, at least he tried, but Colorado and Clover wouldn't hear of it.

Wyatt nodded. A thick lump formed in his throat. He could take a wild guess where this conversation was headed. Gwen had wanted to get pregnant right after they had Michael, and she continued to push during his chemo treatments, but after his death, her desperation to replace their son took over, and Wyatt dealt with it all by volunteering for everything the Navy tossed in his direction.

"I saw her last week, and she's pregnant. I mean like about to pop pregnant."

The air in his lungs escaped, leaving his chest tight and desperate for oxygen. "I'm happy for her," he said, managing to catch his breath. "I know this is what she wanted, and I couldn't bring myself to give it to her, so this is good." He always knew Gwen would move on and have another family. Being a wife and a mother had meant the world to her, only he couldn't be in that world. Not then. Not now. Not ever again.

"She didn't even know you had moved back to town," Clover said.

"I haven't spoken to her since your dad's funeral two years ago." He pulled his hands back and nursed his beer. Gwen would always have a special place in his heart. "I want nothing but the best for Gwen," he added.

"I know. But it bothered me she hadn't thought to let you know."

He ran a hand over his freshly shaven face. "Last time I spoke to her, I told her to go live her life and not to look back. I also told her I thought it was best if we didn't have any communication. Just being around each other brings up too much pain for both of us, and that's not fair to her new husband, and now new family."

"That's about what she said."

"Thanks for telling me," he said. "But you don't have to worry about me. I've come to terms with that time in my life. I've moved on, and," he tapped his temple, "I'm in the game of life."

"Good to know."

He lifted his cell and tapped on the text conversation from earlier. "You mentioned something about your body needing guarding? How much guarding and what does that entail, exactly?"

She covered her mouth and coughed and gasped.

"I take it that was a tongue and cheek comment? Because otherwise it comes off like you might be propositioning me."

Her jaw dropped, but she didn't make a noise.

The front door swished open, and Landon, Hudson, Parker, and Isaac strolled in with big smiles to match their fairly large egos.

"Here comes some of the new crew," he said, waving them over. "Looks like you just got saved by the bell."

"There was no bell, and it was tongue in cheek, and oh Lordy, check out that Landon Asher. He is one hottie."

"He's not my type," Wyatt mumbled. He had no right to allow the pang of jealousy he felt to seep out into the conversation. She was a young, beautiful, sweet woman, and Landon might be a bit of a player, but he was a good man. "But I can see how you might find him attractive. Maybe you should send him some random flirty text."

"Why, Wyatt, are you jealous?"

"No," he said a little too quickly and harshly. "But Landon has some tough baggage. I'm not sure he's the settling down kind."

"Before you all deployed, he went out with Beth. She said he was a total gentleman."

"All sailors are, and he's one of the best, just maybe a little broken." Wyatt stood. "Took you boys long enough. You all remember Clover."

"The singer, songwriter," Hudson said as he slapped Wyatt on the back. "We were just listening to some of her songs on the way over."

"I think you sing them better than the artists who buy them," Landon said. "But we've talked about that before."

"I have to agree." Parker, the youngest member of the team, said as he slid into the booth. "I'm starving and could use some beer."

"I'll send the waitress right over." Clover raised up on tiptoe and kissed Wyatt on the cheek. "I have another set, and then I've been told someone is demanding to guard my body all the way home."

"Damn straight." He cupped her chin and boldly planted a wet kiss on her plump limps. "Play me my favorite."

"Only for you, sailor." She turned on her heels. Her hips swayed back and forth as she maneuvered across the floor.

"Thought you and she were just friends," Landon said.

"We are." Wyatt chugged half his beer.

"Then you won't mind if I ask her out," Hudson said with a chuckle.

"Oh. I mind. And so will our task manager, so back off. Clover is off-limits."

CHAPTER 3

"This is gorgeous. I love it." Clover fingered the silver guitar pendant hanging dangerously close to her cleavage.

"Let me see," Wyatt said, twisting her body. "Wow. It looks fabulous on you."

"You don't have to buy me gifts every time you come home."

"Just carrying on your father's tradition." Wyatt kissed her temple. "Now, you stay right here while I go make sure the house is safe. Got it?"

"Whatever." She shook her head.

He laughed as he practically jogged off down the hallway in his sexy bare feet. Now, all she had to do was get him out of that damn dark V-neck. Jeans, bare chest, and no shoes. Yum. She bit back a sigh as she pulled two red wine glasses down and set them on the counter. "I think you're being ridiculous." After filling the glasses, she made herself comfortable in the family room of her home that overlooked the beach. She'd bought the house right before her father had died. It had been the first thing she purchased after one of her songs hit number one on the country charts. She'd wanted to live on the beach since she'd been a little girl, and it felt damn good to be able to achieve her goals.

She only wished her father were still here, but she knew he was looking down on her with pride.

"I have an alarm that would have gone off and security cameras that would have shown me something," she said. When Wyatt called informing her that he'd been relocated back to Virginia, she went out of her way to help him find a place in the same area.

She never imagined he'd end up renting a house a few doors down. And for the last nearly two years, she'd avoided him, and her feelings. She constantly reminded herself of all the reasons she didn't date military men.

"Safety is far from outrageous, especially when someone sends you an ominous message." Wyatt plopped himself down on the sofa, taking the glass of wine. He swirled the liquid before bringing it to his nose. "I blame your mother for my thirst for fine wine."

"I blame my mom for a lot of things, but mostly for the reason I don't date military men."

"Trisha didn't leave your father because he was in the Navy; she left him because she was jealous of you. She couldn't stand that she wasn't the center of his universe."

"Do you have any idea how fucked up that is? Last year I asked her why she never took me with her to Boston." Clover shifted on the sofa, tucking a foot under her butt. She rested her elbow on the back of the couch, letting her hand cradle her cheek. The sun had disappeared from the sky, leaving a blanket of stars to dance across the dark water lapping at the shore. Her last three songs were written out on her patio while she daydreamed of when Wyatt would return and how she would finally tell him she had feelings.

Her pulse jumped, and her insecurities tickled the back of her mind. Right before her father died, she'd confided in him about her growing feelings for Wyatt. Her father reminded her that Wyatt was a broken man and that would never change because his emotional scars ran too deep and close to the heart. Men like Wyatt didn't do anything halfway, so when they did love, it was all in.

Only Wyatt had his heart trampled on, and she thought he might never give it again.

"Are you going to tell me what she said, or do I have to guess?"

Clover shifted her focus from the foamy water that hugged the sandy beach, to the lights at the bottom of the pool making the liquid dance. "She was testing my father to see if he loved her enough to chase her, but he never came, so she knew she was no longer needed or wanted. Of course, that wasn't true, but my father was tired of her games."

"What about you? What did she say about leaving you?"

"Mostly the same stuff about how my father stole me from her and wouldn't let her see me." Clover shrugged. "But this time, she also told me that she didn't know how to connect with me. That I was too much like my father, cold and distant, and that it was difficult for her to be around me, but that she tried to gain visitation rights."

"Yeah, your mother is a piece of work. I'm sorry."

"She married some guy less than a year after leaving my father. She's got a bunch of stepkids, and she managed to raise them no problem. So really, it was she who never loved me enough."

Wyatt tucked a piece of her hair behind her ear. "I'm sorry." He leaned in and kissed her cheek. "Trisha has issues that have nothing to do with you, so don't take her leaving as a reflection of who you are."

"Now you sound like my grandmother."

Wyatt chuckled. "Elsa cracks me up. I plan on visiting her later this week. How's she liking the nursing home?"

"She's director of activities, and I think she's smitten with a gentleman who just moved in down the hall."

"Why am I not surprised." Wyatt rested his arm on the back of the sofa and stared out the sliding glass doors.

She took the opportunity to examine his strong profile. A few deep-set wrinkles lined the corners of his eyes. Under his chin, he sported a faded scar. His skin appeared soft and freshly shaven, but she always preferred his five-o'clock shadow look.

His full lips curved slightly. "You're gawking at me."

"A little." She swallowed her pounding heartbeat, but it pumped right back up to her throat. "You have a birthday coming up." That had nothing to do with why she couldn't take her eyes off him. "A big thirty-nine." Yeah, it's so sexy to talk about someone getting older. She needed to forget about her nerves and get on with it. "I thought I'd take you to Ronnie's Stake House for a special celebration." God, she hoped she could get a reservation for Friday night.

He raised his glass. "I'll never turn down a steak from Ronnie's, but do we have to call it a birthday celebration? During the training mission, I was constantly reminded that I was the oldest man on my squad. Hell, the next oldest just turned thirty. It feels like forever since I was that young."

"Age is just a number," she said, scooting a little closer, setting the wine on the table. "And you're far from old."

"In ten years, when I'm taking you out for your thirty-ninth birthday, I will remind you of that statement." He batted her nose.

Smiling, she rested her chin on his shoulder. His biceps flexed against her touch.

He cocked his head. "If I didn't know you better, I'd think you might be trying to make a move on me."

"Maybe you don't know me well enough," she whispered with a trembling voice. It became impossible to swallow, and she couldn't tear her gaze away, even though right about now, she wanted to hide under a rock.

Both brows arched, and his lips parted.

But he said nothing.

She held her breath and counted to ten before exhaling. "I'm trying to be subtle." She pressed her breast against his forearm.

His gaze lowered before snapping back up. "You weren't just being funny with those texts? You're hitting on me?"

"I wouldn't call it that."

"What would you call it?"

"More like expressing my feelings and attraction." She kept her gaze locked with his as she angled her head and licked her lips. "Don't you want to kiss me?"

"No. I mean yes. I'd love to kiss you, but no, I can't."

"I see." Well, she just crashed and burned, and thankfully the only person around to witness it was the object of her affection. She pushed away, leaning her back against the armrest. "I'm sorry. I shouldn't have come on to you or flirted with you in anyway. Let's pretend it never happened."

"I can't do that." He downed his wine before

sauntering across the room and filling his glass. He chugged half of that as if it were a shot before standing in front of the sliders with his back to her. "I watched you grow up from this freckle-faced preteen who believed she could do anything, to a confident young woman who took the world by storm."

"Really. Stop. I get it. You're not interested, and I don't need to be embarrassed anymore with some long-winded explanation."

He glanced over his shoulder. "You brought this up, so you need to let me finish, okay?"

She waved her hand. "By all means."

He turned his focus back to the ocean. "You're beautiful, and smart, and everything a man could ever want in a woman. I'd be lying if the thought of us being together hadn't crossed my mind a time or two. But I'm a SEAL, and that isn't something that will ever change."

"I would never ask you to leave the military."

"Then by wanting to be with me, you're breaking your own rule."

"My rules can change."

"My marriage to Gwen failed in part because of my grueling schedule with the Navy as did yours with Reagan. You made that rule up for a good reason. I'm not going to be the one you break it for only to have you regret it later when we don't work out."

"You sound way too confident that we are an impossible couple."

"We are. Just like you and Reagan were. You're the type of woman who wants and deserves the full attention of her other half, and that doesn't happen with military families. You know that better than anyone."

"This is your reasoning for turning me down? Have you seriously forgotten why Reagan and I split in the first place?"

"Because he was deployed all the time."

"Not even close. I broke up with him because he couldn't keep his dick in his pants when he was deployed in exotic locations."

"And if you were to get involved with another SEAL who was shipped out all the time, you'd always be wondering what he was or wasn't doing."

Tired of staring at his back, Clover rose and stepped between him and the sliding glass doors. "You're not that kind of man."

He let out a short chuckle. "I won't argue that point, but you still don't want a man who is owned by the Navy. You've said it a million times."

She nodded, unable to rebut his statement because up until a few months ago, she wouldn't have acted on her desires. Seeing what Keanu and Ainsley had changed Clover's perspective on many things. "Will you answer me something?"

"What?" He rested his hands on her shoulders and massaged gently. Did he even have a clue how his actions encouraged her to continue to try to seduce him?

"How do you feel about me?" she asked.

His eyebrows shot up again. "That is a loaded question with many answers."

She shook her head. "You either care, or you don't. And don't go off half-cocked with all these excuses. Just be honest with me, and with yourself."

He wrapped his arms around her, pressing her head against his chest. "I care very much for you. I always have. You're one of my best friends. We've been there for each other through some serious shit."

Pounding her hands against his firm pectoral muscles, she gripped his shirt. "Stop trying to let me down gently. You don't like me that way. I get it. Now please, for my sanity, can we forget—"

His mouth closed over hers so fast she hadn't realized it was his tongue swirling around inside her mouth. His strong hands smoothed down her back, cupping her ass.

She dug her nails into his shoulders. Her muscles tensed. The kiss grew wild and desperate. A wave of dizziness rolled across her body as he hoisted her up, encouraging her to wrap her legs around his waist.

He stumbled back. "Shit," he mumbled as he fell over onto the sofa, cradling her against his hard chest. He groaned.

"Are you okay?"

"Physically, yes," he managed with a shaky breath. "But my ego has taken a huge hit and might go down in a fiery ball."

Straddling him, she rested her palms on his firm pecs. Her hair flowed, pooling on either side of his body.

He reached out, fanning her face. "I care about you more than I should, which is why I'm going to end this right here. I'm sorry, but we can't do this."

Before she had a chance to register his words, the outside light flashed on, making her squint. Her phone buzzed in her back pocket.

Wyatt lifted her with ease and set her on the sofa. "Stay put." He raced through the sliding glass doors.

He stopped in the middle of her patio with his hands on both hips as he looked left and right.

Her fingers trembled as she pulled up the alert from her beachside security camera. "Wyatt?"

"What is it, babe?" he asked, closing and locking the doors, holding a small box.

She held out her cell. "I've got a blurry image of someone running across my property."

"Whoever it was left you another present." Wyatt set the box on the coffee table. "You call the cops. I'm calling my team."

"For what?"

"Round the clock surveillance."

She blinked. "Isn't that over the top, and don't they have things to do?"

"We're on vacation for a week. They aren't doing anything but drinking and chasing tail. I think they'd rather keep their skills sharp by helping me out."

"Sounds more like you want them around so you will keep your hands to yourself," she said.

"Until just now, I've successfully kept my hands away from you ever since I returned to Virginia. I'm sure I can manage to do it again."

* * *

"What were you doing when the light went on?"

Why did Keanu have to ask that question?

Wyatt's cheeks heated. "Talking." He focused his attention on Clover, who sat at the kitchen table with her laptop, showing Dave all the security camera footage. Wyatt always knew she would be successful at anything she put her hands on. Her restaurant was a thriving business, and he could only guess the kind of money she made on the sale of her songs, but based on the house, she was doing better than average.

"You didn't see anyone?" Keanu asked.

"I already told you that I didn't." Wyatt squeezed his hands together. Had he not been making out with Clover, he would have been more aware and probably would have seen whoever dropped a box on her patio that contained a picture of Clover with a big *X* placed over her face. "But I should have."

"Don't beat yourself up," Keanu said.

"Has Dave said anything to you?"

"Only that the prints they found on the package delivered to the bar don't show up in the system, and every local courier confirms no one used them to bring a package to Clover at the bar." Keanu pointed to the ocean. "Let's step outside."

Wyatt didn't like the sound of that. "What's going on?" he asked as he closed the sliders.

"You called your team, and I know they are out there, even though they are hidden really well. I'm impressed actually. But I want to know what you plan on doing with them?"

"Isaac, Parker, Austin, and Landon have all agreed to take shifts staking out the bar and Clover's house until we have to go back to work."

"What about Lincoln, Hudson, and Bryce?"

"They had plans out of town to visit family. Once they return, they said they'd step up and do whatever was needed to protect Clover."

"Does Clover know you're doing this?" Keanu asked with a cocked head.

"Sort of and she's not happy about it." Wyatt rubbed the back of his neck. "I also called Tex. He said that Cookie and Benny are at the base. They are going to come over so I can pick their brain."

"I'm sure they can add some insight."

"That's what I figured," Wyatt said. "I worry we are all too close to the situation."

"Her dad goes way back with Cookie, Benny, Tex, Wolf, Abe, and Mozart. None of us will sit on the sidelines."

"I know. Tex will be doing some digging, but I

need to ask Clover if he can have access to her computer at work as well as her laptop."

"She's not going to like that."

"No shit, but someone threatened her, twice. And in the same day. Once where she works, and once where she lives. That tells me it's someone she knows."

"Do you find it odd it happened on the day you returned?"

"You think this could be about me?" Wyatt asked.

"I doubt it. But we have to consider the possibility." Keanu took a couple of steps toward the ocean. "Last year she dated this jerk-off from Nashville. All he wanted was a piece of her success as a songwriter. When she broke it off, he flew out here and harassed her. He went away, but I can't help but wonder if he's behind this."

"You told me about him, but you never said what he threatened her with."

"I promised her I'd never tell you, but I'm going to break that promise." When Keanu gave his word, he never went back on it.

Unless it was a matter of life and death.

Wyatt's pulse kicked up.

"He had some naked pictures of her in some compromising situations and threatened to share them with the world if she didn't begin a writing partnership with him."

"Dare I ask where he got the pictures and what they were of, exactly?" Wyatt tensed, bracing himself for the answer.

"Let's just say she was a consenting adult, and she wasn't alone in some of the pictures."

Wyatt swallowed the bile that smacked the back of his throat. "Please tell me she didn't make a sex tape?"

Keanu didn't say anything.

"Fuck," Wyatt mumbled. "What happened to the images, and how do we know they won't come back?"

"I took care of them and made sure he understood what I'd do to him if he ever tried to contact her again."

"Anyone else know about these images?"

Keanu nodded. "I sought the help of Tex, Benny, Cookie; hell, they all know."

"Everyone but me," he mumbled. A couple jogged across the beach with their two puppies. The moonlight danced across the calm ocean. The summer heat prickled Wyatt's skin. "I should stay with her, or maybe she should stay at my place."

"I'm in agreement with you there. If anything

happened to her, Colorado would reach down from heaven and make sure we end up in hell."

"She's not going to like me coddling her," Wyatt said.

"So, don't coddle, but you have to be firm. She might fight you on twenty-four seven togetherness."

"She's pretty shaken up. I'm sure she won't fight too hard."

"Well, while you're spending all this time alone, you might want to tell her how you feel." Keanu slapped him on the back. "It's high time you're honest with yourself, and her. I would suspect she feels the same way about you. Maybe it's time to explore those things."

"I'm not going down that road, and I don't need the distraction while I'm trying to protect her from some crazy stalker."

"I'll agree that you don't need any distractions, but you're head over heels for her. You might as well stop fighting it and see where it takes you. And I know for a fact, her father would approve, so don't let that stop you." Keanu turned and pulled open the sliders. "If I were you, I'd stay here. Her security system is better than yours, and it won't throw the stalker off, making it easier to catch him."

"I don't plan on leaving her side."

"That means sleeping in the same bed."

Wyatt growled. "I'm not having this conversation with you." Reluctantly, he made his way toward the kitchen where Dave and Clover continued with their conversation. Wyatt snagged a glass of water and leaned against the counter. "What did we miss?" he asked.

"We've compiled a list of three people that might want to harm Clover," Dave said. "We have the waitress she fired, though so far her story checks out. The ex-fiancé, Reagan, but we don't know what the motive would be since there doesn't seem to be ill will on his part. We have an ex-boyfriend from Nashville, which is our best bet, if you ask me. And a neighbor across the street who doesn't like that Clover fenced in her yard where he used to cut through to get to the beach instead of using the public access. Another good possibility."

"That's a start," Wyatt said, pinching the bridge of his nose. He'd talked the neighbor down when he'd helped put the fence up with the no trespassing sign. He was a bit hot under the collar, but he didn't make Wyatt jittery. "Keanu and I were talking, and we've got a buddy in the private sector who is a master at finding people. His skills would benefit the police where your hands might be tied or you don't have the manpower."

"As long as you're not standing in my way, then I'll take all the help I can get. I think that's it for now." Dave stood. "We'll have a car drive by when possible but keep your security system engaged and don't hesitate to call. I'll be in touch as soon as forensics has had a chance to examine the box and image."

"We appreciate it," Keanu said. "I'll walk out with you." Keanu kissed Clover on the cheek before shaking Wyatt's hand. "Let me know what Tex finds out."

Wyatt nodded.

Clover glared. Her lips drew into a tight, angry line. The room filled with dense air.

Wyatt jumped when the front door slammed shut. "Why am I getting the evil eyes?"

"You called Tex," she said matter-of-factly. "Why would you bring him into this?"

"Because he's the best at what he does, and I think he should take a look at your digital imprint and poke around your computer to see if he can find something we're missing."

"I don't like letting anyone into my personal computer, much less my business one," Clover said.

"Tex isn't just anyone, and you know you can trust him."

"I know. I'm just struggling with all that is going on. I don't understand why this is happening to me."

"I'll get to the bottom of it, I promise." Wyatt placed his hands on her shoulders and gently massaged, hoping he'd help alleviate some of the tension he sensed building inside her muscles. Of course, he was about to create some new tension, but it had to be done now. "We need to talk about what happened before the motion sensor was tripped."

She folded her laptop. "I'm listening."

He opened his mouth but couldn't find the words. He cleared his throat, but nothing happened. This shouldn't be so damn fucking hard.

"Cat got your tongue?"

"You're not making this easy by glaring at me with an angry expression."

"I'm not angry. I'm confused by your actions which don't match your words."

"Fair enough," he said. "Let me start with the fact that I'm attracted to you and not just your pretty face and killer body, but you. Everything about you. I think about you way too often."

"I don't see what the problem is," she said.

"I'm not handling this well. But the bottom line is I care very much about you, but we can't be anything other than friends."

"And why is that, exactly?" she asked, letting out a long sigh.

"I've done the marriage and family thing, and all it did was nearly kill me."

"Wyatt, you—"

"Let me finish," he said sternly. "I understand I didn't cause my son's cancer and that we did everything we could possibly do in order to save him. I almost went broke doing it, and in the end, it destroyed my marriage. I do get that if there were a next time, things might not go down like that, but for me, there are no second chances when it comes to love and family. I can't do it again."

"I'm not asking for you to put a ring on it. I'm just asking for you to be honest and explore these feelings we have."

"I'm being completely honest." He pulled out a chair and straddled it. "Ever since I moved back here, I've thought about what it would be like to be with you, but it's purely sexual, and I won't lead you on like that. I know you, and someday you want marriage and the baby carriage."

She opened her mouth, but he shushed her with his forefinger.

"I'm a SEAL, and until the US Navy tells me I'm no longer fit to do my job, that's never going to change. It's who I am, and I can't give you what you deserve."

"Are you done?"

He nodded.

She cupped his cheeks and brushed her lips over his, sending a warm shiver across his body. "I'm not the reason you are sidestepping what is growing between us. You're using me as an excuse, so you don't have to face your fear of being hurt again."

She palmed his mouth. "Ever since Michael died and you and Gwen divorced, I've watched you build this gigantic wall. But your heart craves love, yet you fill it with the adrenaline rush you get from your job instead of what you want most as a man." She let her hand drop to her lap. "I put myself out there, and you don't want me. I accept that. But you need to dig deep inside your soul and understand why you pushed me away." She stood, giving him a quick kiss on the cheek. "I'm going to bed. I know that you're not leaving, and I'm not too stupid to live, so I won't fight you on that. Feel free to pick whatever guest room you want. I'll see you in the morning."

As soon as she left, he dropped his head to the table. Every word she spoke had been the truth.

But it didn't change one damn thing because he knew, deep down in his heart of hearts, he'd break hers in two if he let anything happen.

He wouldn't be able to live with himself if he caused her any pain.

And he didn't want to think about what it would do him if he loved and lost again.

CHAPTER 4

"Well, look at what the cat dragged in." Clover rushed to the front of the bar and wrapped her arms around Cookie. She'd known him since she'd been in diapers and loved him like family.

He lifted her up off the floor and twirled her around like she was a little girl. "You are a sight for sore eyes."

"Hey. Where's my loving?" Benny asked with his arms stretched wide. "I'm starting to feel under-appreciated."

"I would never." She gave him a big squeeze. "I hope you didn't come into town because of what happened to me yesterday." She showed them to a table, glancing once over her shoulder, thankful that Wyatt must still be in her office doing...she had no idea what, other than avoiding having to be in her presence. The last twenty-four hours had been more awkward than when she'd called her father to stop at the drugstore to get her tampons, and Wyatt ended up delivering them.

She'd been fourteen and mortified.

"We have Navy business at the base, but we wouldn't blow into town without stopping by and seeing our favorite famous songwriter."

"I'm not famous," she said as heat spread across her cheeks. "The singers who record my songs are who make them special."

"You have the same humility your father had." Cookie nodded. "He was a good man."

"The best," she said softly. "I take it Wyatt has brought you up to speed?"

"He did." Cookie took her by the hands. "He's worried about you."

"To be honest, I'm a little scared myself." She understood that Wyatt cared deeply. And now she knew he found her attractive. That he'd even thought about her in a sexual way. That was great, but he was right about one thing. She didn't want him in her bed for a brief but satisfying romp in the sack. If he couldn't even commit to trying a relationship, then she really didn't want it. Now she had to figure out a way to go back to being his friend so the awkwardness would stop.

She shouldn't have opened her damn mouth to begin with.

"Not that we're happy that you're frightened, but we are glad to see you taking this seriously," Cookie said. "You've always been a stubborn, independent woman."

"I still am, but I'm not stupid," she said. "My mom thinks I should take a trip to visit her."

"You've got to be kidding me." Cookie cocked his head.

"I don't trust that woman as far as I can spit," Benny said. "Why did you call her anyway?"

"I didn't," Clover admitted. "She called the restaurant looking for me, and Chris told her." She held up her hand. "Before you go off on Chris, he doesn't know the dynamic between me and mommy dearest."

"What the hell did she want?" Benny asked.

"She said she just called to say hello, but I suspect she wanted money or for me to introduce someone to some music executive. Ever since my first song hit the charts last year, she's been up my ass pretending to care about me and my career, but I know better."

"I'm sorry your mother is a loon," Cookie said.

"Let's focus on the issue at hand." Benny leaned back in the booth, stretching out his arms over the back cushion. "Tex is looking into your ex-boyfriend from Nashville. What was his name?"

"Conrad Smith," she said, folding her arms across her chest. "He started off as a really nice guy but got way too possessive, and I did call the cops on him when he showed up at my home. But I haven't heard a peep from him since, and that was over six months ago." She resented having her life under the microscope, even with men she trusted.

"Why'd you break up?" Benny had been one of many SEALs who showed up at her doorstep, offering their help and support, and she'd forever be indebted to each and every one of them.

So, she couldn't lie, no matter how embarrassing.

"He really only wanted me for the connections I have in the music business. Once I figured that out, which wasn't soon enough, he got weird. He showed up at my house making demands. He threatened me."

Cookie and Benny exchanged a sideways glance.

"Oh shit. You know, don't you? Does Wyatt know?"

"No," Cookie said.

"Please don't tell him." She turned her gaze

toward the door leading to her office. "He'll go batshit crazy."

Cookie leaned across the table and curled his fingers tenderly around her wrist. "I guess Wyatt never told you about his little sex tape."

Her mouth dropped open. Heat flushed her cheeks.

"So you know," Benny said.

She nodded.

"He, of all people, would understand. Trust me on that," Cookie said.

She swiped at her face, brushing the tears that had escaped her eyes. "I spent all of last night racking my brain over who would want to hurt me, and Conrad is the only one I can come up with."

"Conrad and your mother."

"My mother might be a passive/aggressive bitch who would toss me under the bus if it meant she got ahead, but she has no reason to threaten me. Besides, if it were her, she'd be by my side pretending to protect me. That's just how she operates."

"That's true," Benny said.

"Don't you worry. We'll figure this out and handle it. In the meantime, you can't fight Wyatt on anything. He can't protect you if you go rouge," Cookie said.

"I'm scared enough to agree to having him on my six all damn day," she said as Chris stepped from behind the bar and waved. "I've got to get back to work."

"Are you going to sing today? We sure do miss that voice of yours," Benny said.

"I'll do a set after I take care of some restaurant business."

"Awesome," Cookie said. "And if you see anyone or anything that doesn't seem right, let us know so we can investigate. We'll be here through the dinner hour. After that, we have to head back to the base."

"I really appreciate you being here." She kissed both of them before scurrying across the main dining room.

"They look familiar. Who are they?" Chris asked with his hands planted on his hips and his eyes narrowed with a disapproving glare.

"Friends of my father and Wyatt."

"So, they are SEALs," Chris said with a hint of distaste hanging on his words. "I take it they came to protect you."

"Those two? Nah. They had business at the base this morning. They always stop by when they are in town."

"Well, the good news is that all these brawny men

are probably scaring off the stalker." Chris inched closer, taking her hand. "Wyatt told me what happened at your house last night. I know he believes staying there with you is protecting you, but maybe you should consider going where no one will expect."

"Such as?"

"My place."

She opened her mouth, but he continued talking.

"I know I'm not on the beach, and my townhouse is like a third the size of your house, but it's a gated community so no one can come and go. That would also free up Wyatt to put his skill set to better use if I was with you all the time. And before you go on about putting me out, or inconveniencing me, you wouldn't be. Really, it's the least that I can do."

She patted his chest. "I appreciate the offer, but for now, I'm staying put. I'm not letting some psycho chase me out of my own house. Besides, Wyatt has the entire week off."

"Well, if they haven't caught the bastard by then, or you change your mind, the offer still stands. And if you need anything at all, I'm just a phone call away."

"Again, thanks, but Wyatt has it under control."

"I've got your back, too, you know." Chris smiled.

"I know." For good measure, she gave him a hug. "Your friendship means the world to me."

He held her a little too tight. "Here comes Wyatt. I better get back to work," he whispered against her ear, his lips brushing against her skin in an intimate gesture.

She would have to make sure Chris understood, once again, she and him were never going to happen.

Kind of like Wyatt had done with her.

* * *

Wyatt put on his best fake smile while he watched Chris get a little too hands-on with Clover. By the way she crinkled her nose, she didn't appear to welcome the kiss on the cheek, nor the hands on the small of her back. However, Wyatt kept a safe distance. It wasn't his place to meddle in Clover's life, outside of keeping her safe, and Chris was harmless enough. Wyatt knew that based on Tex's report into Chris background.

Nothing stood out.

The man didn't have a scratch on his record. Not even a juvenile infraction, something that Wyatt had to beg to have removed from his history so he could join the Navy.

Besides, Wyatt had known Chris for a good five years when he'd started out as a waiter when Clover's father owned the Sans.

"Wyatt. Do you have a minute?" Chris called as he practically jogged toward the middle of the restaurant.

"Sure." Wyatt stopped and turned. "What's up?"

"I know you're really good at your job," Chris said, glancing over his shoulder. "I also know you'd never let anything happen to Clover, but I was thinking she might be better off staying at my place. The neighborhood is gated, and we have security cameras everywhere. That would give you more time to go out and find whoever is behind these threats."

Wyatt forced his initial gut reaction to the back of his mind. Even if Chris was using this situation to hit on Clover, he did have a point about his neighborhood, but Wyatt wasn't about to leave her alone with Chris.

"Thanks for the offer, but I'm not a cop or a detective. I'm a sniper, and my skill set is best utilized as Clover's protector. Wherever she goes, I go, and I doubt your townhouse is big enough for all of us."

Chris frowned but quickly recovered by nodding as if he understood.

"Anything else?" Wyatt asked.

"Yeah, but I never told Clover this."

"Tell her what?"

"A month or so ago, I saw that guy she was dating from Nashville," Chris said.

Wyatt groaned. He didn't have time for secrets. "Here? At the Sans?"

"Yeah. He showed up looking for Clover. It was when she went north to go visit her aunt. I didn't tell him where she was, but I did tell him if he didn't leave, I'd call the cops."

"And he just left?" Wyatt had a hard time believing that Chris could scare anyone off, especially if Keanu's threats hadn't done the trick.

"He gave me something to give to Clover." Chris lowered his gaze as he pulled a small envelope from his back pocket. "Obviously, I never opened it or gave it to her."

"She's going to eat you for lunch." Wyatt took the thin paper between his fingers and slapped his palm.

"I was hoping you would have thought I made the right decision."

"Bringing it to me, yes. That was the right move. But she's still going to be pissed as hell when she finds out you've been sitting on it for over a month. Now if you will excuse me, I need to meet with my friends." Wyatt turned on his heels, not giving Chris a chance to continue the conversation.

"Glad you could join us." Cookie slid across the bench. "What have you been doing?"

"Watching video surveillance from the restaurant and Clover's beach house." Wyatt snagged a glass and poured himself a beer. "The woman that fits the description of courier didn't have a package with her when she entered the bar, but her purse was big enough to hold one."

"Do we know who the woman is?" Benny asked.

"Not yet. Tex and the cops are working on it. Once we have an ID, Dave will hunt her down and question her, but in the meantime, Chris just handed me this." Wyatt pushed the envelope across the table. In big bold letters was: *Clover Sullivan* written across the top. "He said her ex-boyfriend from Nashville dropped it off a month ago, but he took it upon himself to make sure she didn't get it, much less ever know that asshole had come back to town."

Benny's gaze darted between Wyatt and Cookie.

"What's going on?" Wyatt asked.

"She asked us not to—"

Wyatt raised his hand. "I know about the

pictures, and I'm smart enough to keep that information to myself."

"Good, because she's embarrassed enough, and to have you know would just make her feel even worse about the entire thing." Cookie took the envelope and held it up toward the light. "But I have a hard time believing Conrad would show his face in here after all that went down."

"Me too. She does keep a backup of all her video surveillance, so I can pinpoint the time she was visiting her aunt and look for Conrad in the footage," Wyatt said.

"Do you have any reason to believe Chris would lie about something like this?" Benny asked. "Other than the obvious crush he has on Clover?"

Wyatt shook his head. "What do you both think about opening the—"

Cookie ripped open the envelope. "You really should stop thinking so much. It interferes with..." Cookie held a piece of paper. His eyes grew wide, but then narrowed into tiny little slits. "Well, fuck me," he mumbled as he slammed the paper over, covering up whatever was on the other side.

"What is it?" Benny asked.

Wyatt swallowed.

"Looks like not all of those images were destroyed, unless she made new ones," Cookie said.

"What the?" Wyatt reached out for the paper.

"No. You don't want to go there," Cookie said in a dark tone.

"Fuck off and give it to me."

Cookie leaned back, raising both hands. "I warned you."

With shaky fingers, Wyatt carefully lifted one of the corners. "Jesus." He tilted his head, not wanting to expose too much, considering she was totally naked, except for some nipple squeezing apparatus and a whip, which she used to smack the ass of some dude bent over her knee.

"What are you looking at?" The sound of Clover's voice made him jump, but he made sure to fold over the paper.

"Nothing," he said.

"Bullshit. Whatever it is, your face is bright red," she said.

"Sit down, please." Benny scooted over. "We need to talk."

"I don't like the sound of that," she mumbled as she slid into the booth, her gaze bouncing between Wyatt and the damn stupid naked printout in his hands. He wanted to see her body in all its wonderous glory, but not printed on a piece of paper by a printer that was obviously low on ink.

"We were recently informed that Conrad paid you a visit last month when you were at your aunt's," Wyatt started, doing his best to keep his rage in check. It wasn't directed at her, because she hadn't done anything wrong, but he could see himself unleashing his wrath in front of her, and he couldn't have that. "And he left you an envelope."

"With a message," Cookie added.

"There was a message on the picture?" Wyatt asked.

"What picture? What message?" Clover asked with narrowed eyes. "And Conrad was here?"

"One question at a time," Cookie said. "There was handwriting under the picture. I didn't get to read it all, but it said something to the effect of: *you can't hide from this anymore.* But there was more."

She raised her hand and pointed her finger at the paper now pressed against Wyatt's chest. "Let me see."

"Come stand behind me," Wyatt said.

"Why?" she asked.

"Because I can't have you destroying this, and you will want to. Not to mention you won't want anyone else viewing this."

"Shit." She covered her face with her hands. "I thought Keanu destroyed them all." Her voice trembled, taking away it's sweet tone and turning it into something dark and ugly.

Wyatt was going to enjoy putting his fingers around Conrad's scrawny little neck and squeezing the life out of him. "Wait," Wyatt said. "We've all made mistakes, but Tex made sure every digital imprint was gone, and Tex doesn't make those kinds of mistakes. Could this be a fake?"

"You saw it. You tell me," she said, brushing her wild mane from her angel-like face.

"I saw your face and a boob, and since I've never seen you naked, I have no idea." He cocked a brow. "Promise you won't rip it to shreds."

She nodded.

He pushed it across the table.

She sucked in a deep breath and slowly lifted the paper off the table. Bending forward, so no one else could see, she eyed the image.

The longer she stared at it, the more Wyatt's fury swirled around in his gut.

"Oh, thank God," she said with a long breath. "That's not me. I mean, it's my face but not my body, and that sure as hell isn't one of the pictures Conrad and I took."

"How can you tell?" Wyatt asked.

"For starters, I would never want to whip someone's ass, nor have I ever in my life worn a nipple pincher. I have a tattoo under my right breast. That body doesn't, and all the photos that Conrad and I took, it showed off my tattoo. She's also wearing earrings. I can't wear them, not even clip-on ones. They hurt my ears. And finally, my pinky toe is a bit mangled since I had a bone removed from it two years ago, and her feet are flawless."

"You got all that from only looking at it for a few seconds?"

"I know my body," she said.

Wyatt swallowed, hard. "What does the writing say?"

"You can't hide from this anymore. I'm going to ruin you." She folded the paper and handed it back to Wyatt. "Conrad did want to destroy my career, but he's stayed clear of me since Keanu had spoken to him."

"Well, maybe he's been waiting until the time was right to strike," Cookie said. "We're going to need to send that picture to Tex."

"And the cops," Benny said.

Clover shrugged. "It's not my body, so who cares."

"I care," Wyatt snapped.

Benny stood. "I think I'll hit the head."

"I'll make like a girl and follow you," Cookie said.

Wyatt breathed in through his nose and let it out the same way, like a raging bull.

"Why are you acting like a lunatic? That's not me in that photograph."

He splayed his hands wide and focused on his breathing and not the pounding rushing between his ears or the wave of nausea floating around in his gut. "Besides having to prove that image is a fake, it serves as a reminder that you took—"

She waggled her finger in front of his face. "Don't you go judging me. It's not like you and Gwen didn't have a sex tape, and don't deny it."

He closed his eyes for a brief moment. "How did you know about that?"

"I was with Grandma when Gwen accidentally gave it to her, thinking it was the birthing video."

Wyatt dropped his head to the table, letting his forehead smack the counter hard. "You've got to be kidding me."

"You've got a cute dimple on your ass."

He bolted upright. "How much did you—"

"Less than thirty seconds, but Grandma managed to click on the middle of the file, hoping to get to the good stuff, and boy, did you put a smile on that old bird's face."

"I will never be able to look at her again without dying of embarrassment," he mumbled, rubbing his temples. "But the difference here is Gwen never used that to hurt me, and thank God, it's been destroyed."

"Thank you for caring about my honor and dignity, but as long as we can prove that's not me, I don't really care who sees it."

He nodded. "Sorry I overreacted. It's just that this whole naked selfie thing wigs me out. Gwen wanted to do it, but I couldn't, and I didn't know she recorded us until after, and I wouldn't do it again."

"For the record, neither would I. Well, the sex tape that is. Naked selfies, that's a different story. What's the big deal between two people who care about each other?"

"You cared about Conrad and look at what that got you."

"I didn't love him," she said. "And for the record, if Conrad set foot in this building, I would have known. Not a single person that works here doesn't know what he looks like or that he's not welcome here."

The hair on the back of Wyatt's head stood at attention. "Are you calling Chris a liar?"

She shrugged. "I don't know. The only way I believe Conrad came in under the radar was if he came when Chris was the only one here, and that doesn't happen often. However, if I was out of town, it's highly probable." Her eyes grew wide. "He opened a note that was meant for me?"

"No. Cookie did that," Wyatt said.

"Doesn't make me feel better. Why didn't Chris give it to me?"

"I'm guessing that he was trying to protect you. He's in love with you."

"No, he's not. He's got a thing for some new redhead."

"That redhead?" Wyatt pointed across the room.

Chris leaned against the bar while he rested his hand on the redhead's forearm. His smile was as big as the state of Texas.

"That's the one. And look at the way he's talking to her. See, not overly interested in me."

"I think he's trying to make you jealous, but that's neither here nor there. I'm going to have someone watching him, just in case."

She tilted her head. "Why, Wyatt Jackson, I think you're the jealous one."

"Only if he'd seen you naked, and then I'd be more than jealous and would have to kick his ass."

"What if I told you he has seen me without my clothes on?" She batted her lashes over her sparkling eyes like a little devil daring him to lose his cool.

"Please tell me you're only saying that to get a rise out of me."

"I tried to get a *rise* out of you last night, but some stalker asshole ruined my fun." She leaned in. "Tell me, Wyatt, would you have had the control to stop me had we not been interrupted?"

"No."

She opened her mouth but slammed it shut right quick.

"I might have been a little hasty in turning you down." He stood, lifting her off the seat and heaving her to his chest. Out of the corner of his eye, he could see Cookie and Benny pause by the hallway, but more importantly, Chris kept his gaze in their direction.

He knew he was being childish, but he didn't care. He was like a wolf marking his territory, only she didn't belong to him.

And she never would.

But Chris wasn't good enough for her, plain and simple.

"Excuse me?" She fisted his shirt as if to push him

away but changed her mind. "Don't be a dick and a tease."

"I'm not teasing," he whispered right before he brushed his lips over her sweet mouth.

Her body relaxed into his like melting chocolate. A hum vibrated against his throat as she let out a small moan.

"I've got to get a hold of Tex, and I'd rather do that at your place than here. Are you ready to go home?"

"I promised Cookie and Bennie I'd sing."

"Tell them to go download one of your songs, and you can sing for me privately while I wash your hair in the tub." What the hell was he doing?

Getting her out of his system, that's what.

CHAPTER 5

"I want to take a swim." Clover stood in the doorway of her office wearing a bikini and a mesh cover-up, doing her best to look sexy, but she wasn't sure she'd pulled it off.

Wyatt glanced up over her laptop and coughed. "That doesn't leave anything to the imagination."

Ever since they left the Sans, Wyatt had been abnormally quiet. He'd barely said five words the entire ride home and only managed to grunt a few more once inside.

Deep down, she knew he wasn't serious about washing her hair in the tub, much less taking her to bed. He'd been overprotective with her before when she'd been a teenager, so why would he be any different now that she was an adult?

"Am I allowed to go for a swim?"

"As long as I'm with you." His fingers pounded the keyboard before he shut it closed. "Let's go."

She let out a puff of air. "Do we have any news about anything?" On the way past the linen closet, she snagged a couple of towels. Not once did she glance over her shoulder, but she didn't have to. She could feel his hot breath on the back of her neck as he followed so close she thought he might climb right up inside her.

"I've got some information, both good and bad," he said, pulling open the sliding door. "There is no way to prove the image is a fake from the printed version we have, other than you discussing your body. But, given the case history, the cops in Nashville will be questioning Conrad. They are working on getting a search warrant for his computer and any digital hard drives he might have."

"That's progress." She tossed her cover-up over a chair. Standing at the edge of the pool, she dipped her toe into the refreshing water. Bending her knees, she pushed off the side and dove in. Warmth coated her skin. She turned and kicked toward the surface. "What else?" she asked, swimming to the side, resting her arms on the concrete.

Wyatt sat with his legs dangling in the pool,

kicking them gently back and forth. He reached out and brushed her wet hair over her shoulder. "Tex found out that Conrad has had three women file restraining orders against him over the last six years. All for stalking. One woman told the police that he broke into her house and cut up her collection of stuffed animals."

"That's crazy."

Wyatt nodded. "Everything points to him, and we know he's in Nashville." He kept his gaze on the water as he swirled it around with his feet. "But one thing doesn't add up in my book."

"What's that?"

"Dave picked up the woman that dropped off the box. She was paid a few grand by a woman to deliver the package."

"What woman? The waitress I fired?"

"That, we don't know yet, but how would the waitress and Conrad be connected?"

"Conrad knew her pretty well. She flirted with him like crazy, but she flirted with all the customers to get good tips."

"Another thing I don't understand is why wouldn't Conrad just leak the photographs?"

"I can think of one reason," Clover said, letting her body lean against his powerful thigh. "He wanted to be a writing duo. Partners both in and out of bed."

Wyatt growled. "I don't want to know about your past lovers."

She laughed. "I know way too many of yours. That one chick with the really big fake tits comes in every once in a while, asking for the Stud Muffin."

He batted her nose. "For the record, I never slept with her."

"Seriously?"

He nodded. "Not sure if this matters at all, but Chris took the redhead back to his place."

"Good for him. Now maybe he will leave me alone."

"One can only hope," Wyatt said with an amused smile. "She was a real looker." He placed his fingers in his mouth and whistled.

"Pig." She splashed him before taking ahold of his legs and giving him a good tug.

"Shit," he mumbled as she submerged him completely under water. He popped up, shaking his head like a dog. "You are so lucky I left my phone on the table." He grabbed her by the arm and yanked.

She wrapped her arms and legs around his strong body. "Why do you resist the idea that we could be good together?"

He sucked her chin into his mouth, nibbling a little. "In the long run, we are horrible for each other. I'm exactly everything you don't want in a man and you're—"

"What you don't want in a woman," she finished for him.

"That wasn't what I was going to say." He hoisted her up to the side of the pool, wrapping his arms around her waist and resting his cheek on her thigh. His hot breath ignited her skin. "If I were the settling down kind of man, you are everything I'd want in a woman. But I'm not that man, and all I have to offer you is a fling, and I'm terrified our friendship won't last if we do that." He pressed his lips against her inner thigh before pushing himself out of the pool. He snagged a towel and rubbed his hair. "I can't risk destroying our friendship, no matter how badly I want to make your toes curl."

"Wyatt, how do you know anything unless you give us a try?"

He tossed the towel over his shoulder and smiled. "I know we'd end up breaking each other's hearts, and I won't have it. Sorry that I've led you on. Now, I need to go shower. Don't do anything crazy like skinny-dip. I've got eyes on the house, and while they are all good men, they will look. I mean, I'd look."

Quickly, she put on her cover-up and glanced around. "Where? Are they inside too?"

"Just outside and you don't need to know where they are. I pulled out some steaks from the freezer. After I shower, I'll cook you dinner, okay?"

Hugging the towel, she glanced toward the roof, half expecting to see some dude in fatigues pointing an Uzi in her direction. She did a full three-sixty, trying to find signs of any of his men.

"My guys are the best. You won't find them." He laughed as he stepped inside.

She stood by the pool and stared into the house. Wyatt had gone to one of the guest rooms to take a shower.

Which meant he would be naked.

And she wasn't going to let him off the hook that easily.

* * *

Wyatt stood under the showerhead as cold water pelted his body. He pressed his hands against the cold tile and let the spray douse his back. Goose-bumps covered his skin, but he didn't care. He needed the chill to keep himself from doing something crazy like…

The door swished open and in stepped a very naked Clover.

Her wet hair cascaded over her chest. Her nipples peeked out between the strands. Water beaded down her tanned body.

He reached out and traced the clover tattoo under the swell of her breast. "What are you doing?" he managed between ragged breaths. He blinked, trying to stop from staring, but he couldn't peel his gaze away from her enchanting physique.

She reached out and twisted the nozzle. "Shit. Do you always take such chilly showers?"

"Do you always walk in on men taking a shower?" The warm water didn't help the growing desire swirling in the pit of his stomach.

"Only the ones I'm trying to seduce."

He swallowed.

Hard.

"We've talked about why this is a bad idea," he croaked out.

She took the bar of soap and lathered it up in her hands. "You might have, but I don't agree. And right now, you're not doing anything to stop me." She spread her fingers over his chest, digging her fingertips into his muscles.

He grabbed her wrist.

He should stop her.

He should put a towel around her body and send her back to her own room.

He should do anything but kiss her.

Except that is exactly what he did. And it wasn't a tender, soft kiss. No. He rammed his tongue between her lips on a search and destroy mission. He held her so tight that his back slammed into the shower wall. Water rolled across her skin, helping his hands find every sweet swell of her body. He molded her muscles as if she were a pile of warm, wet clay that needed to be sculpted into pure perfection.

She tossed her head back and moaned while he dabbled kisses down her neck, heaving her full breast into his mouth. The room spun, and he became intoxicated by her rosy scent and her sweet nectar.

He made sure not a single inch of her went untouched.

Clutching at his head, she rolled her hips in unison with his mouth. She loved like no other woman he'd ever experienced. She gave herself completely and without reservation.

Greedily, he took it all.

Her climax erupted with the force of a twister, spinning his raw emotions until he'd lost all control.

He lifted her into his arms and shut off the shower. Setting her feet on the fluffy white floormat, he turned her back toward him and stared at her in the mirror. Her gaze tore through him like a raging fire consuming the woods.

His chest tightened, and he found it difficult to breathe as he slid himself inside.

Her lids fluttered over her cool-blue eyes. Her hands gripped the sink as she rocked back and forth.

Wrapping his arm around her middle, he rubbed her hard nub in a slow feathery motion. He wanted to bring her pleasure over and over again. He wanted her to feel desired. Sexy.

Loved.

His heart pumped harder and faster.

"Wait," she whispered.

"What's the matter?"

"Nothing. I just want to face you." She turned and jumped up on the sink. Wrapping her arms and legs around him, she drew him inside.

His muscles went weak, and he had to grip the counter to keep from falling to his knees.

"Yes," she said with a breathy moan, her face buried in the side of his neck. Her stomach quivered against his like the waves of the ocean crashing into the shore.

He gritted his teeth and held on for as long as he could. Taking her mouth with a passionate thrust of his tongue, he let himself go, shuddering his own release.

The sounds of their groans mixed together like the powerful music of the opera, stirring up all his emotions and tossing them to the wind.

Holding her tight, he smoothed her wet hair and kissed her exposed shoulder. He cupped her cheeks and searched her gaze for answers to questions he didn't know he had.

Her eyes twinkled under the LED lighting, and her smile sucker punched his ability to form any coherent thoughts, much less words.

He cleared his throat. "That was unexpected."

The right side of her lips curved higher. "That's all you got?"

He chuckled. "Unexpectedly wicked."

"That's a little better." She patted his shoulder,

slipping from his embrace and wrapping a towel loosely around her waist. "Eyes up here, sailor."

He growled. "If you cover them up, I might be able to look somewhere else." He forced his gaze to her angelic face. His heart dropped to his gut. Not only had he had sex with Clover, but he'd done so like a wild animal in heat.

She tossed him a towel. "I'm hungry and I want—"

All the outside lights flashed, and the alarm screamed through the night air.

"Fuck," he mumbled. "Where are your clothes?"

"In the bedroom," she said, clutching her breasts.

"Let's get them on and go find out what's happening." Quickly, he hiked up his jeans, not bothering with anything else other than his weapon. "You ready?" he asked, stepping into the guest room just as she pulled a shirt over her chest. Her nipples puckered through the fabric. "You don't have a bra?"

"I do in my room."

"We don't have time for that," he mumbled, snagging his phone.

One missed called.

Four texts.

All from Landon.

Landon: Perimeter breach north side. Parker checking it out.

Landon: Lock cut at side gate by pool.

Landon: Parker on the move.

Landon: If I don't hear from you in two minutes, I'm coming in.

Wyatt hit the call button.

"It's about time," Landon said.

"What's going on out there?" he asked.

"The neighbor, Joe Hickey, broke the fence, and we caught him spraying weed killer in all her bushes. He also has a package that he said a woman gave to him to leave by the pool."

"What's in the box?"

"A couple more doctored naked pictures with *payback is a bitch* written all over them."

"Call Keanu and the cops. We'll be down in a minute." He laced his fingers through Clover's, giving her hand a good squeeze. "What other old boyfriends have you sent naked pictures to?"

"Now you're being an asshole." She yanked her hand away.

"Let me rephrase. Who else might know about the pictures in order to use them against you?"

"No one that would use them to hurt me…except

my mother," she said with sarcasm dripping from every word.

"You told her about what happened with Conrad?"

"Conrad sent her a couple right before he tried to blackmail me. He thought she'd put them all over the internet."

"Shocker that she didn't considering that might put her in the limelight."

"I'm forever grateful she didn't."

"Did she ever give you a reason why she didn't?"

"Something to the effect of protecting my reputation, which is bullshit, but she wouldn't gain anything long term from sending the photos to the media."

"Have you gotten in a fight with her lately? Anything weird happen between the two of you?" Wyatt asked. Trisha had been known to do some crazy things. A few of which her daughter hadn't ever been told about, and for good reason. He tugged Clover toward the split staircase. While the siren had been turned off, all the lights around the house were still as bright as the sun.

"As a matter of fact, I have."

"Care to enlighten me?" He paused in the middle of the staircase and held her gaze for a long moment.

"She wanted me to help my stepsister break into the Nashville scene. I told her I'd introduce her to a few people, and I might even be able to get her a set at one of the bars on Broadway, but I couldn't get her a record deal like she wanted."

"That would be more than enough to set off Trisha." He rubbed the back of his neck. "Is your stepsister any good?"

"I have no idea. I've never heard her sing, and honestly, I couldn't pick her out of a lineup if I tried. I haven't seen any of them in like eight years."

"Your mom can be vindictive."

She narrowed her eyes. "She can be."

"You know how she went off half-cocked whenever she thought your father was having an affair. She even once slit his tires after following him to the Sans."

She poked Wyatt in the chest. "Tell me something I don't know."

"You have to promise not to get mad at me. I was under strict orders to never tell you, and you were like only fourteen when it happened."

She cocked her head. "From fourteen to sixteen, I didn't once go visit my mother. She would call crying, saying that my dad was keeping me from her, but my father said it was complicated and that my mom was going through some things. Since my mom was always having issues, I let it go. But from the look on your face, something happened."

"She threatened to kidnap you, and on more than one occasion, she showed up. Your father had her arrested once after she broke into the house."

"Are you talking about the time some whacko came in and stole my Barbies…oh shit. That was my mom?"

"Holy fuck. I forgot she stole all your dolls."

"You don't really think my mother would do this, do you?"

"Do you remember your seventeenth birthday party and how late your father had been?" Wyatt hated doing this and not just because he was breaking a promise he'd made to her father, but because he knew it would mess with Clover's psyche.

"There had been a problem on the base, and it couldn't be helped."

"But we all showed up on time," he said with a raised brow.

"Would you please just get to the point."

"Your mother showed up, demanding to come to your party. She said she wanted to start over with you, but he knew better and all she wanted was either the Sans, money, or both."

"Ever since Daddy died, she's been on me constantly about the bar and how it should have been hers, among other things."

Wyatt kissed her forehead. "I think we found our stalker."

She shivered. "My own mother. I should have known."

CHAPTER 6

Clover stared at her mother's contact information blinking on her cell phone screen, almost daring her to hit the little phone icon. The last time she'd called her mother had been when her father had been killed. The conversation hadn't gone well, not that she'd expected her mother to all of a sudden behave like a parent, but she hadn't expected her to ask if her father had done the right thing and left her the restaurant. But what really hurt had been the words that followed.

"Well, we can be business partners. It will be fun, and it will be good for your little sister. She wants a singing career too, so it will give her a place to try out her new songs."

Over Clover's dead body would that happen, and

she let her mother know it.

That resulted in her mother calling her a few choice words and then hanging up on Clover.

"How are you holding up?" Wyatt asked as he stepped into her bedroom. He closed the door and sauntered closer.

"Not well," she admitted, taking his hand as he joined her on the edge of the bed. "My mother might be a loon, but I'm struggling with this master plan to destroy me. I mean, she's my mother. She's supposed to lift me up, not bring me down."

"If I hadn't been there when she planned on kidnapping you, I wouldn't have believed any of this either, but it makes total sense." Wyatt ran a finger across the side of her face and through her hair. "Do you remember when the first song you sold hit number one?"

A smile tugged at her lips. "Of course I do. It was an amazing day, and you and Daddy made it even more special by throwing that impromptu party for me."

"Until your mother showed up and tried to ruin it," Wyatt said. "I was horrified by how she tried to steal your thunder. And every time something magical happened in your life, if she wasn't given credit publicly, she shit on you."

"She once went as far as to call a press conference to discuss my career. She actually said she helped me write my songs but wouldn't dare take the acclaim since that's what mothers do. I've learned to ignore her over the years."

"And that's the problem. You live a humble life, and you don't make a big deal over your success. So much so, you won't even go to awards shows or be interviewed. You don't allow yourself the fun of being recognized for your talent because your mother makes it ugly for you. But in turn, your ability to avoid the limelight makes your mom nuts. If she doesn't know what you're doing, or which songs are yours, she can't use your gifts in order to get her fifteen minutes of fame."

"It's hard to believe she would go to such lengths. I have to ask myself, what's the end game? What's she getting out of this?"

"Have you called her? Asked her to come down and take care of you? Knowing her, I bet that's what she's looking for. It's like that woman on one of the Real Housewives going along with a cancer scam because she wanted her friends to bring her a casserole."

"I'm terrified that not only did you reference a

reality television show, but that you might have actually watched one."

"When I went to visit my sister last summer after her surgery, she made me binge-watch a season with her. Dumbest thing I've ever seen," he said. "And yet oddly, highly entertaining. But my point was that your mother will do anything for attention."

"This still seems over-the-top outrageous."

He took her chin between his thumb and forefinger. "We should have confirmation in the morning."

"I would love to be the one to confront her. Or at least be in the room to hear her excuses." Her mother had a slew of reasons why she'd been a horrible mother, most of which were bullshit and only meant to take the focus off her mother and put it on someone else. God forbid her mother ever take responsibility for her own actions.

"It's best we let the cops handle this." He raised her hand and kissed the back side.

"What if we're wrong and it's not her?" She fell back on the bed and stared at the skylight. Big puffy clouds floated across the star-speckled sky. The white moon glowed in the black night. "What if I do have some crazy psycho stalker who wants to chop up my body, put it in a plastic bag, attach a cement block to it, and toss it into the ocean."

"The only person who is going to do anything to your body is me." Wyatt positioned himself on top of her.

She accepted his weight and wrapped her arms around his shoulders. Lifting her head off the pillow, she puckered her lips and brushed them over his soft mouth. She had no shame in his arms. "I might let you have your way with me."

He groaned, burying his face in her neck. "This is such a bad idea."

"It doesn't feel too horrible to me." She rolled her hips, feeling his hardness press against her body, sending heat waves drizzling all over her skin like molten lava. "Actually, it feels spectacular."

"You know that's not what I mean," he whispered as he rolled to his side, splaying his large hand over her tight midsection. "I shouldn't be doing this." He palmed her breast, pinching her hard nipple between his thumb and forefinger.

"And yet, you are," she panted out in short breaths. Her chest heaved up and down, increasing the pressure from his hand. "Just admit that you care about me."

"I never said I didn't, but soon, my team will be deployed, and I will be gone for God only knows how long. You're young and have so much ahead of you, including a family and children, but I can't give you those things."

"When are you going to realize that you're only hurting yourself by keeping that wall built up around your heart?"

"That has nothing to do with your future." He flopped to his back and tossed his arm over his eyes. "Besides, I don't have a wall," he said softly. "My heart is open and exposed. But I won't put myself or anyone I love through that hell again."

She pried his arm from his face. "Not every child dies of cancer, just like not every SEAL is a cheater. Don't you see that you're not living and that existence without substance is nothing more than a shell of a life? I'm not asking for the moon and the stars. I'm asking for you to give us a shot."

He cupped her face and drew her in for a deep, passionate kiss, but he broke it off the second she tried to slip her hands under his shirt. "I can give you friendship. I can even give you sex. However, there is no us, and there never will be. I'm sorry, but my heart doesn't have any love left in it. Not to give, much less to accept."

With as much grace as she could manage, she stood and smoothed down the front of her nightgown. "You're a fool," she said.

"Probably."

"You can tell yourself that the love train has left the station, but you know deep down that you're too afraid to open your heart and let it happen. You're a coward." She turned on her heels, but he grabbed her by the arm and twisted her around. "Let go of me."

"I'm not a coward," he said behind gritted teeth. "How dare you belittle my feelings like that."

"No one is putting down your pain. I held your hand during Michael's treatments. I was there for you the day he passed. I stood next to you and Gwen at the funeral, and I held you when you cried after Gwen left. I know the kind of man you are, and the kind of love you have to give." She pressed her hand firmly in the center of his chest. "This aches to feel something again, but you won't let it because you're scared it might hurt. Well, guess what? Life is messy. It's ugly, and it's full of sorrow. But it's also wonderous and packed full with new adventures, and I'm not talking deployments."

He pushed her hand away. "It's best I walk out of this room right now. I'm sorry I hurt you."

"I knew what I was doing when I stepped into that shower, so don't worry about me. I'll be okay because I know if you aren't going to come around and admit how much you care about me and want to be with me, then there is someone else out there who will. You see, my heart is open to love, as well as the pain that love might bring."

His lips parted, but no words came out.

She padded across the bedroom and opened the door. "Good night, Wyatt."

"Good night," he mumbled and marched out into the hallway.

Careful not to slam the door, she eased it closed and slid to the floor, covering her eyes. The tears came quick and hot.

But she would get over Wyatt because she was a fighter, a survivor, and her father's daughter.

* * *

Clover sat on the steps to the beach and blew into her steaming mug of coffee. The sky turned a light blueish-orange color as the sun started to peek out over the ocean.

By the time she'd gone to bed, it had been two in the morning. She had no idea where Wyatt had slept. She told herself she didn't care but having some young hot SEAL on Wyatt's squad give her a message that Wyatt had left the building. Tears pool in the corners of her eyes.

Wonderful.

Landon jogged up the beach, making his way toward the deck. "How are you holding up?" he asked.

"I'll be better once someone confirms my mother is the one fucking with me."

"That's rough." Landon leaned against the railing. "Wyatt went to go chat with some chick they believe is the girl who has been giving everyone these boxes to deliver. He's hoping that will help confirm or not that your mother was the culprit."

"That's what Parker said." Clover closed her eyes and inhaled the bitter coffee scent. "How old is that boy anyway?"

Landon laughed. "I think he just turned twenty-three."

"He looks like he's twelve."

"Don't tell him that. He's a little sensitive, especially since we all started calling him baby."

"That's just mean," she said with a slight laugh. "How are things with you and Beth?"

"She's a nice girl, but she's not for me, and I don't want to lead her on." Landon shrugged. "You know this lifestyle makes it difficult to maintain relationships."

"That's a cop-out, and you know it."

"No. It's a reality. I mean, do you really want to spend the rest of your life with a man who is deployed more than he is home?"

"Actually, there is one that I would consider doing that with, but he's got more hang-ups than I do."

"Well, now, that's interesting." Landon pushed from the railing and plopped himself down on the steps. He leaned back on his elbows and stared out toward the water. "So, the rumors are true."

"What the hell are you talking about?"

"You and Wyatt," Landon said with a stupid grin.

"What about us?"

"From day one, it was made crystal clear to the entire platoon that Clover Sullivan was off-limits, and anyone caught sniffing around would be dealt with by unpleasant means."

She arched a brow while her heart fluttered out of control. "By who?"

"Wyatt. That's who. He told each of us that he didn't want to hear about his team hitting on you and that he'd have our hides if we did. He says he doesn't have feelings for you. That he's just respecting your father's memory, but it's obvious to everyone else he's madly in love with you and either he's too stupid to go after you, which I doubt is the case. Or he's utterly terrified, which I know is true, but no one can say anything to him without having our heads ripped off."

"Love is too strong of a word to describe our relationship, which is funny, because we don't have one," she admitted.

Landon was close to her age, and they had become fast friends the second he walked into the Sans. Since then, they had become sounding boards for each other. But she shouldn't be talking about his team leader and her desire to be with him in a forever kind of way.

But she needed someone to talk to.

"Do you want to tell me what happened?"

"It's not so much what happened as how what happened changed our friendship. I shouldn't have let things go this far. He's right. We're horrible for each other."

"Wyatt is probably horrible for everyone except you." Landon chuckled. "You bring out the best in him. We all see it. Even Keanu has made a comment about it."

"Wonderful. You're all talking about us. That's really going to piss Wyatt off."

"He only gets mad because he knows we're all right, but for whatever reason, he doesn't believe he deserves you, or some such shit. Have you told him exactly how you feel?"

"Pretty much. But he thinks I want him to give up being a SEAL because I swore I'd never date another one, and he has his own baggage."

"Never say never." Landon waggled his finger. "But I suspect this has more to do with him than you. Some people describe SEALs as fearless men, but that's not true. We've had to learn to push our fear deep in our gut and only use it in situations where we need to stay alive. Fear is a good motivator that way, but not so much when it comes to matters of the heart. He's going to say he doesn't want to hurt you, but in reality, he's afraid to take that kind of risk. It's worse for us to do that than to parachute behind enemy lines in the middle of the night while being shot at."

"That's good insight, but with Wyatt, it goes deeper than just having loved and lost."

"I know," Landon said. "I lost a child too."

"What?" She snapped her gaze in his direction. "I'm so sorry. I had no idea."

"It's not something that pops up in casual conversation, but one night during training, Wyatt found me huddled up under a tree with a picture of my daughter. I can usually keep my emotions to myself, but it would have been her fourth birthday and that just always gets me."

Clover reached out and took his hand. "I can only imagine."

Landon nodded. "My late wife—"

"Late?" Clover swallowed her pounding heartbeat.

"My wife took her own life, and our baby's."

Clover gasped, chocking on the air filling her lungs. "Jesus," she whispered. "That's horrible."

"It is. I still blame myself sometimes. I knew Linda had mental illness, and I didn't do enough. The morning she killed herself, she had me believing she had this big breakthrough in therapy and how things were just going to be better from that point on, but it had all been a lie. It's left me wondering if I could ever give my heart to another woman again. Right now, I know I can't, but watching Wyatt struggle with allowing himself to love again makes me realize that closing yourself off from the possibility is no way to live."

"And yet, you blew Beth off."

"I said I realized it, not that I was ready for it." Landon jumped to his feet. "If you love Wyatt, you'll fight for him, no matter what he says or does. You both deserve to be happy." Landon pointed toward the house. "He's back. I better go and find out if I have new orders, or if I'm staying put on beach guard duty."

"Thanks for sharing with me. It means a lot."

Landon nodded.

Clover continued to sip her coffee as she watched the waves gently lap at the sand. Most of her good childhood memories were with her father and grandmother, not her mother. For a long time, she believed if she'd only been a better daughter, her mother might have loved her more. Even today, that thought constantly seeped into her mind and soul, making her doubt her own ability to love another human being.

But she knew none of that was true. Whatever her mother's issues were, they had nothing to do with Clover.

"Hey you," Wyatt said.

She jumped, spilling the last of her coffee. "I didn't hear the sliders open."

"Sorry. Force of habit to be as quiet as possible." He set a box on the table and snagged a chair and made himself comfortable. He ran a hand over his scruffy face. "The police have finished questioning your mother."

"And?"

He shook his head. "It's not adding up to be your mom anymore."

"Why do you say that?" She clutched at the necklace dangling toward her breasts. It would serve as a constant reminder of what could have been had Wyatt been able to get his head out of his ass and take a risk.

"They can't find any evidence. She has a solid alibi, and according to the local police, she was genuinely shocked." He reached in his back pocket and pulled out her cell phone. "She's called you ten times, and I believe there are text messages as well."

She narrowed her eyes. "Where'd you get my phone, and why are you spying on me?"

He laughed. "You left it in the kitchen by the coffee machine, and if I were spying, I would have asked Tex to unlock it remotely."

Ignoring the sexy man smiling at her with a smug look, she unlocked her cell and pulled up her mother's messages.

Mom: What on earth is going on down there? And why would you think I had anything to do with it?

Mom: I can't believe you would think I would threaten you. I'm your mother.

Mom: I hope you're proud of yourself. Your stepfather

had to explain to your little brothers and sisters why Mommy had to go to the police station.

Little brothers and sisters? Had her mother finally lost her marbles? First, all of her stepsiblings were over the age of eighteen and only one still lived at home. Second, she barely knew her mother's husband or his kids. Not that she had anything against them, but she'd never really gotten to know them.

And at this point, she didn't think it was a good idea.

Mom: And for the record, I was never going to kidnap you or hurt you, ever. Your father used you as a weapon in our divorce, and since I left, he wouldn't let me have custody. He also wouldn't let me see you. Numerous times I had to threaten to take action. But I lost because he had the world snowed about him being a decent person when in reality, he was just an asshole doing his best to punish me and take away the one thing that meant something to the both of us. You. I will never forgive him for that.

Mom: Still, in death, your father is brainwashing you against your own mother. I hope they catch whoever is threatening you. I really do. But it wasn't me, and I'm desperately hurt you would even think I could.

"Did she write a letter or what?" Wyatt asked.

She copied all the texts and sent them in a

message to Wyatt. "I just sent them to you so you and Keanu can show them to whoever."

"Good." Wyatt lifted his leg, resting his ankle over his knee. He clasped his hands behind his back. "Tex is doing some digging to make sure we can officially rule out your mother."

"Thought you said the cops already did that and that you don't believe it adds up?"

"Until someone is in custody, everyone is suspect."

"So, I take it you'll be spending the day and night with me again."

"If you rather, I can have one of my men hang inside with you while I take up surveillance outside."

"Considering what happened and the fact that things are just way too weird between us right now, maybe that's a good idea."

"Consider it done." He stood. "Do you have a preference?"

"I'm probably the most comfortable with Landon," she admitted.

"Of course you are."

She stared at his back while he slipped back into the house.

"Well, that went well."

CHAPTER 7

Wyatt perched himself on the back patio with a mug of coffee in one hand and a gun in the other. He glanced over his shoulder. Clover sat in her living room with her guitar. Her fingers plucked away at the strings while Landon relaxed on the sofa, listening intently.

Being jealous wasn't an emotion Wyatt understood, or welcomed.

And he knew he had no reason to think Landon would ever consider trying to take Clover to bed. Although, he had no right to stand in his way if he wanted to because Wyatt had successfully sabotaged any possibility of something between him and Clover.

And that was for the best.

Or so he told himself.

The sliders opening caught his attention. Keanu stepped out into the moonlight. "I should beat the crap out of you."

"It's nice to see you too," Wyatt said, raising his mug.

"Why the hell is Landon inside with Clover? And don't give me this shit about you being more comfortable waiting to shoot someone because I know Hudson is back in town. Specifically, he's right over there where you should be if you had really taken Landon's spot."

"Clover and Landon are the same age and good friends. I figured she'd have a better time with him than me." Wyatt kept his gaze fixated on the darkening sky and not the glare of his task manager.

"What did you do to piss her off?"

"Maybe I'm the one that got bent out of shape," Wyatt said.

"Okay, Pinocchio."

Wyatt downed the last few sips of his lukewarm coffee, wishing he'd put a little kick in it. The burning in his throat slithered down to his stomach. "Why are you here?"

"I was at the neighbor's house. A cop is with him

doing a sketch of our suspect, and I wanted to ask Joe a few questions."

"And?" Wyatt glanced over his shoulder and grimaced at Clover, who sat a little too close to Landon while she gave him a lesson on how to strum a guitar.

"The old man was a little more forthcoming this time around with answering questions, and he admitted that the woman who hired him asked him to do property damage, but he was the one who came up with killing off her landscaping so he could see the ocean better."

"What did this woman give him in return for his troubles?"

"Five grand, which is about the same as the chick who delivered the broken Barbie doll."

Wyatt arched a brow. "No way in hell is Trisha parting with that kind of cash."

"I agree. Besides, Tex checked into all her banking, and no sizeable amounts of money have been taken out. I'm confident it's not Trisha," Keanu said.

"Whoever it is knows her mother stole all her Barbies and that she and Conrad made naked images and videos."

"That leaves me, you, Cookie, Benny, Tex, and the rest of the gang, and we both know none of them did it." Keanu rested his arms on the table and leaned forward.

Bang! Pop! Pop! Bang!

"What the fuck?" Keanu muttered as he hit the deck.

"Go inside with Clover." Wyatt flattened himself on the ground. He tapped the mic in his ear. "Landon, report," he said calmly.

Keanu nodded as he made a beeline for the door.

Wyatt glanced over his shoulder. Landon and Clover were nowhere to be seen.

"Safe," Landon said.

"There is movement on the beach," Parker said.

Pop! Pop! Bang!

White flashes of light appeared in the darkening sky where the ocean and the sand merged.

"That's not gunfire," Wyatt said.

"It looks like teenagers with firecrackers," Parker said.

"I'll go check it out. Cover me." Wyatt slowly rose, keeping his weapon at the ready. "It's wide-open space between me and those kids."

"We've got your back," Isaac's voice came over the speaker. "I've got them in my sights, and it looks like they are bringing out some bigger fireworks."

Stupid-ass kids.

Wyatt jogged up the beach and not directly at the flame igniting what he assumed were fireworks, but one never knew. "What the hell are you doing?" he yelled.

The boys stopped laughing, dropped the firestick, and took off running.

"Oh no, you don't," Wyatt yelled, raising his gun and pointing it at the moon. He pulled the trigger, and the teenagers stopped dead in their tracks.

"What the hell, man?" One of the boys turned, holding his hands up. "Weren't you expecting the fireworks?"

"If you really thought that, then why did you run?" Wyatt tapped his earpiece. "I need backup, and someone call the locals."

"We were told we were surprising someone with it," one of the boys said as he took a couple of steps back. "Don't you live in that house?"

"You're trying to tell me that someone told you to set off fireworks in front of that house?" He stole a glance toward the house as Parker and Isaac jogged in his direction. Landon and Hudson flanked out to the north, waving as if he was onto something.

"Dude. You have to let us go," one of the boys pleaded. "We only did what someone paid us to do."

"Who paid you?" Wyatt asked, eyeing the three boys.

One of them couldn't be older than fourteen. He stared at Wyatt with wide, fearful eyes. The other two looked to be maybe sixteen or seventeen. The one that spoke sported a man bun and kept looking around as if he were afraid someone was going to come out of the ocean and gobble them all up.

"We didn't mean any harm," the man-bun kid said.

"Just answer me, and things will go better for you when the cops get here. Now who gave you the fireworks?" Wyatt asked.

"Locals will be here in five." Parker circled around the other side of the boys.

Isaac went right for the fireworks, making sure the flames were put out.

"Please. Let us go," the youngest boy pleaded. "My parents are going to kill me."

"You could have killed someone, including yourself." Isaac held up one of the tubes holding the fireworks. "This shit is old as dirt, and I can tell this one is faulty. It could have blown up in your face."

"Are you ready to talk?" Wyatt asked.

"Some lady gave us a few hundred dollars each to set off this stuff down here."

Wyatt's pulse sped up. "What lady?"

"We don't know. Just some woman who was hanging out in the park down the street," the man-bun kid said.

"What did she look like?" Wyatt asked as the speaker in his ear crackled. He raised his hand and tapped the device. "Keanu?"

What sounded like a cough echoed. "Clover," Keanu said weakly. "Taken."

"Fuck." Wyatt kicked the sand. "Isaac stay here. Parker, you're with me." Without another word, Wyatt sprinted toward the house. He blinked, making sure he kept his focus laser sharp. He leaped over the railing and nearly tripped over one of the reclining chairs as he made it to the sliding glass doors. "Clover? Keanu?" he yelled.

Someone coughed behind the counter in the kitchen.

Wyatt's heart sank to his gut. He rounded the corner and dropped to his knees. Ripping off his shirt, he wadded it up and put pressure on Keanu's abdomen.

"I'll check outside," Parker yelled.

"They got..." Keanu coughed.

Wyatt leaned down and pressed his ear to Keanu's chest. "Take it easy, buddy. It sounds like you might have a punctured lung." Wyatt took a peek at Keanu's wound. "Knife?"

Keanu nodded. "They took Clover."

"Did you get a good look at them?" Wyatt asked.

"Redhead," Keanu said with a rattle.

"The chick that's hanging out with Chris?" Wyatt asked.

"Yes," Keanu breathed his answer. "And Chris."

Parker came through the front door. "Whoever took her is gone."

Wyatt forced his fear to the back of his mind. He needed to focus on developing a plan. He needed to find Clover before it was too late.

* * *

Clover folded her arms over her chest and stared out into the ocean. "What the hell is going on?" she asked, but it was more of a rhetorical question, and she didn't expect Keanu to answer.

And he didn't.

He stood stoic by the sliders. Knowing him, he wanted to be out there in the action, instead of babysitting.

She shivered.

"Can you hear them?" she asked.

"I don't have a wire, but I can see them, and it all looks fine."

"Who do you think is behind all this?" she asked, rubbing her aching temples. This was not how she thought she'd be spending this week with Wyatt home. Of course, she never really expected him to sleep with her, but it happened.

And now she wasn't sure if she regretted it or not.

No. She would never feel bad about having a night with Wyatt, but it would take some time for her heart to get over it.

Maybe she should take a long trip to Nashville. Chris could run the restaurant, no problem. And she could spend some time putting her emotions to a song or two.

"My money is still on Conrad." Keanu turned. "I need to use the bathroom. I'll be right back. You stay away from the windows. As a matter of fact, why don't you follow me down the hall and wait for me by the door." She took two steps before something snagged her hair, pulling her back. "What the..." She gasped as a metal object flew through the air, landing right in the center of Keanu's gut.

He groaned, dropping to his knees.

"Keanu!" Clover tried to race to his side, but someone yanked at her hair harder.

"What the fuck did you do that for?" a man asked. "No one was supposed to get hurt."

"Don't do it, old man," a female voice said as she lunged forward, letting go of Clover and kicking a gun out of Keanu's hands. She reached down and yanked out the knife.

Clover sucked in a deep breath and turned to run. "Chris?" she asked with her mouth gaping open. "What are you doing here?"

"Let's go," the woman said.

Clover blinked, staring at long red hair. "Janice?"

Janice pushed the bloody knife against Clover's neck. "Time to go, sweetheart."

"I'm not going anywhere..." The cold metal scraped against her skin.

"No need to hurt her." Chris pushed the knife away. "Don't make me regret that."

She swallowed the sob that loomed in her throat. Her body twisted and jerked as he tugged her out the front door. Her heart hammered in her chest. Cold metal closed around her wrists.

At least she knew Keanu wouldn't be alone on that floor for long. Wyatt and his men would go inside, and they would find him She had to believe that.

Chris shoved her into the back seat of a light-blue crossover car with a black leather interior. He climbed in behind the steering wheel while Janice twisted her body in the passenger side, keeping a gun aimed right for Clover's heart.

The car bucked left and right. Her body slammed against the door. Her shoulder throbbed. She blinked, doing her best to note every turn.

Pay attention to your surroundings. Her father's words rattled in her mind.

She took a quick peek over her shoulder as they pulled onto the main road heading off the island and toward Norfolk.

"I can't believe you stabbed him. That wasn't part of the plan," Chris said.

"Maybe not yours, but it was always part of mine." Janice waved the bloody knife around as if it were a magic wand.

"If he dies, you'll go to jail for murder," Clover said. "And if he lives, you're going to jail for other things."

"No, I won't," Janice said with a sinister laugh. "Chris here might, but I'll be free and clear."

"What the hell does that mean?" Chris snapped

his head. The car swerved into the other lane. A loud honk echoed in the night. "The plan was to scare Clover into my arms, not kidnap her, much less kill anyone." He glanced over his shoulder.

"If you weren't supposed to take me, then why am I here?"

"I only wanted you to see how good I am for you. How I will protect you. Those boys on the beach were just supposed to draw Wyatt and his men out, leaving you alone so I could come in and save the day."

"You really are a dumbfuck," Janice said. "You really believe they would leave her all by her little self?"

Clover continued to take in slow, deep breaths. A million things bounced around in her brain, but she couldn't make sense of any of it. She needed a little time and for them to keep talking. When she'd been a little girl, she used to laugh at her father and the way he'd teach her how to defend herself. Or what to do in dangerous situations.

Right now, all that training gave her confidence that she'd manage to come out of this mess standing. First, however, she needed to understand the situation, and that meant remaining calm.

Chris pulled into a townhouse complex in a

decent part of town. He pulled the vehicle into the garage. "I didn't mean for this to happen," he said as he helped her out of the SUV. "You were supposed to come with me willingly. I just wanted you to know how much I love you."

"That's not love," Clover mumbled, turning her attention toward Janice, who stood at the door with her fingers curled around the knob. "What was or is your plan?" Clover asked.

"It's not really my plan. Why don't we let Mother tell you." Janice smiled. "I told her you wouldn't recognize me, but she made me dye my hair anyway."

Clover blinked the tears stinging in her eyes. "Jenny?" she asked. The last time she'd seen any of her stepsiblings had been a good eight years ago.

"No. I'm Julie, but close enough." She pulled open the door, and there stood her mother, with her arms wide and a bright smile.

"Hello, darling. So glad you could join us," her mother said. "Being your mom is going to finally pay off for me. You, on the other hand, not so much."

CHAPTER 8

The last time Clover had laid eyes on her mother had been at her college graduation. Her mother hadn't bothered to attend the ceremony, but instead showed up at the party her father had planned. Her mother then proceeded to cause a scene, accusing her father of horrible things, as well as implying that the original music that she created during her years in the music program had been stolen.

"Cat got your tongue?" Her mother stepped to the side.

Clover swallowed the bile that slammed into the back of her throat. No matter what, she had always tried to keep the lines of communication open with her mother. She hoped that one day her mother might magically change. "After all those text messages, telling me what a bitch I was for thinking it could possibly be you, and well, you lied. As if I should have expected anything else."

"You've always been too much like your father."

"I'm proud of that fact," Clover said, puffing out her chest. "And damn grateful I'm nothing like you."

Her mother raised her hand and slapped Clover across the cheek.

Clover's body jerked, and her arm caught the blade in Julie's hand. "Fuck," Clover muttered. She glanced down at the cut. It wasn't horribly deep, but it hurt like hell.

"I don't know what the two of you have going on," Chris said. "But this isn't what I signed up for, and I'm not going to stand here and let you hurt Clover like this." He curled his fingers around Clover's forearm. "Let's get out of here."

Julie shoved Clover aside, and with a flick of her wrist, she had managed to disarm Chris.

"You're not going anywhere, and if you try something, I'll let Julie kill you," Clover's mother said.

"Let me? I thought that was part of the plan, that I was going to get to draw blood." Julie waved the gun in the air before pressing it against Chris' temple. "He's done his part; now we can be rid of him."

"I have a few more things in mind for him." Clover's mother turned and walked into a small kitchen. She took a seat at the table and ran her hands over a stack of papers. "We need to make this look all realistic, and since he's in love with Clover, we might as well have them meet their death together."

"You're not going to get away with this, Mother." Clover tugged at the metal wrapped around her wrists. "Wyatt is going to make sure you pay for this."

"You and all your father's little cronies. Well, this they will lose, and I will win." Her mother shoved a piece of paper across the table. "Sit, child."

"No."

Thud!

She glanced over her shoulder only to see Chris buckle to the floor, landing on his knees.

Julie stood over him. "Try to run again and you will get a bullet between the eyes."

Reluctantly, Clover did as her mother requested. "What is it that you want?"

"That's easy. I want what is mine. Your father took my career as a singer and that bar from me. He turned you against me and then used the talent you inherited from me for his own riches. He didn't really care about you, only what you could do for him."

"I think you have your identities screwed up because that is your MO, not Dad's." Clover scanned the document in front of her. The words: *Last Will* jumped out at her. "What is this?"

"Your new will that leaves me all your music, including what you've written but haven't sold to do with what I want. You're also leaving me the bar."

"No one is going to believe I would do that," Clover said.

"It doesn't matter what they believe; your signature will be authentic, and I will mourn your death in style," her mother said.

Julie stuck a key in the handcuffs and released them. "If you try anything, your death will be so slow you will be begging me to end your life."

"Here's a pen; now be a doll and sign," her mother said.

"I'll sign if you tell me a couple of things," Clover said.

"Yeah. What's that?"

"Why bring Chris into this?" Clover stole a glance at Chris who sat cross-legged on the floor, rubbing his bleeding head.

"That's funny because this was all his idea," Julie

said. "I had come to town to scope things out for mother, and I befriended Chris to see what I could dig up."

"You used me," Chris mumbled.

Julie kicked Chris in the chin with her heel.

He flopped over backward with blood oozing from his lips. "Fuck," he said, holding his face.

"That wasn't necessary." Clover squeezed the pen between her fingers.

Julie grabbed her by the hair and yanked her head back. "Keeping talking, sister, and I'll put my heel through your nose."

"Well, Mom," Clover said. "You certainly raised her right."

"Bitch," Julie mumbled before she took the gun and smashed it against Clover's cheek.

Clover groaned, cupping the side of her face.

"Don't get blood on the will." Her mother snatched the papers. "Julie, really dear. Calm down. You will get to kill them both, I promise."

"And how are you going to explain my death, especially to all the Navy SEALs that were at my house? And the one with a hole in his gut who knows both Julie and Chris." Clover resented the rattle in his throat and the slight tremble in her hand. She needed to keep her fear in the back of her mind, like Wyatt had taught her when she'd been too afraid to get on a horse when she'd been fifteen. He told her that fear was a good thing and that she could channel the wasted energy fear created and use it to accomplish great things.

Right now, she'd settle for staying alive.

"Chris is going to kill you," her mother said.

"I would never do such a thing."

"But you've been stalking her, and you kidnapped her with the help of some woman who doesn't exist and will disappear. But during the abduction, things went terribly wrong, and you were forced to kill her," Clover's mother said. "Afterward, you are overcome with such guilt and grief that you take your own life."

"Do you have any idea how crazy that sounds?" Clover asked, but as insane as her mother's plan was, it was also ingenious and if Wyatt didn't figure it out soon, her mother might actually get away with murder.

* * *

"You didn't have to come," Wyatt said. "But I'm damn glad you did."

"Our work at the base was done, and our flight

out isn't until the crack of dawn, so we might as well make ourselves useful." Cookie held up his weapon and checked it over.

Benny secured his protective vest. "I get the little bitch who stabbed Keanu."

Landon, Hudson, Parker, Austin, and Isaac all suited up in silence.

Wyatt took a step back, holding in the raw emotion that threatened to explode. "None of you have to be here, and honestly, we all know we could get in trouble for not letting the locals handle this."

"Don't insult us by asking that question again," Benny said.

"Well, we better get a move on before they put it all together," Wyatt said. "Tex can only hold them off for so long."

"Radio check." Cookie tapped his earpiece. "Count off."

"Check," Wyatt said. He listened intently as everyone's voice boomed between his ears.

Benny made a swirling motion with his hand, and Landon, Parker, and Austin flanked to the north side of the condo. Benny would perch himself in the large tree in the side yard. Parker and Austin would take the back, and Landon would climb up on the roof.

"Go," Wyatt commanded.

Hudson and Isaac flanked off to the south, and Cookie slinked across the road and stationed himself in the bushes in the front of the house.

"I count four people," Cookie whispered. "I can only verify the redhead and Chris, who is on the floor, bleeding pretty bad."

"We know Chris and the redhead took off with Clover, so who could be the fourth person?" Benny asked.

"I wish I knew," Wyatt breathed out his response. "Anyone else got a better view to what I'm walking into?"

"I see two women sitting at a table. Clover is facing me, but I have no idea who the other woman is," Parker said. "Clover appears calm, and she's looking at some paperwork."

"What about weapons? What do you see?" Wyatt asked as he tucked his gun in the side holster and made his way up the sidewalk. It had been years since he'd worked with either Cookie or Benny, but he trusted them with his life.

And after a month of intense training with his new team, he knew he had the best in the business covering his back.

"The redhead has a handgun, and there is a

bloody knife on the table. Actually, it's only about seven inches from Clover's hand. The unknown female has a handgun on the chair next to her. That's all I see," Parker said.

"Same," Benny said.

"I've got a clear view of the perimeter," Landon said.

Wyatt's phone buzzed. He yanked it out and glanced at the text quickly. "I just got a text from Dave asking what the hell I'm up to. He's got a local heading to the hospital to question Keanu. Unless anyone tells me otherwise, I'm ringing that bell."

"Let's get your girl," Cookie said. "So, you can make nicey-nice—"

"Silence on the radio unless necessary," Wyatt said, not wanting to hear about how he's screwing up with Clover.

He probably lost his chance with her, but when this was over, he'd beg for another opportunity to prove to her he could open his heart again.

All the curtains had been drawn in the front of the house, and Wyatt didn't spot any movement. He didn't know if that was bad or good. Making a fist, he pounded on the door and then rang the bell. He wanted to make sure he was heard, so he repeated the knock, this time even louder.

"Who is it?" Chris' voice filtered through the thick door like a small child's whisper.

"It's Wyatt. Let me in."

"I'm sorry, but I'm sick and not up to company," Chris said.

Did the idiot think they didn't know he'd taken Clover? Maybe they thought they had killed Keanu.

"It's about Clover. She's missing, and I need your help." That ought to stir up some trouble and force Chris to reconsider opening the door.

"She's not here," Chris said. "Now please leave."

"I can't do that, Chris. Now let me in before I shoot my way—"

"No. Just go. You have to go. If you don't, I'll be forced to call the police," Chris said.

Fuck this. "I'm going in hot," he whispered.

Before anyone could respond over the wire, he kicked in the front door.

Chris tumbled backward, holding his head, and he fell to the floor, landing with a loud thud and a groan. "You really shouldn't have done that." He pressed his hand against an open wound. His lids blinked over his glossy eyes. "She's going to kill you."

"Who is going to kill me?" Wyatt asked, holding his weapon steady.

"I am." The redhead appeared in the hallway holding a gun.

"Who the fuck are you?" Wyatt inched closer to Chris, sizing up the damage to his body. He had a few bruises to the face along with a gash and good-size egg over his right eye. His complexion had paled, and it looked as if he might pass out at any minute.

"Julie."

"That means nothing to me. Now get that thing out of my face, or I'll kill him."

Julie laughed. "If you really want to, go right ahead. I won't stop you."

"But you might not want to do that," a woman's voice echoed through the townhouse.

"Holy shit," Wyatt blinked once, making sure his eyes weren't playing tricks on him. "I didn't want to be right about you." He swallowed, staring at Trisha holding a gun to her own daughter's head. Bile reached from the bottom of his gut to his tonsils. He coughed. "So, it was you all along."

"I can't believe I'm going to have to have you killed too," Trisha said, shaking her head. "You are one fine specimen of a man. Too bad you drank my ex-husband's Kool-Aid."

Wyatt locked gazes with Clover. "Are you okay?"

She nodded with big eyes. "Keanu?"

"He's just fine." Wyatt gave her a slight smile. "Pissed off he's not here saving the day, but he's going to live to give me shit for this, and for not telling you how I really feel, for the rest of my life."

Clover's mouth curved into a sweet smile. "You want to express your undying love for me now?"

"Oh, my God. Shut the fuck up. No one cares, and you're all going to be dead as soon as you sign your new fucking will." Trisha grabbed Clover by the hair and shoved her face into the wall before yanking her back toward the kitchen.

Wyatt growled and took a large step forward, but Julie stepped in his way, shoving a gun in his gut.

"No funny stuff, or the girl gets it first, got it?"

Wyatt nodded as he offered a hand to Chris, yanking him to an upright position. "He needs a doctor."

"He needs a medical examiner because in a few minutes, you're all going to be dead."

Wyatt helped Chris into a chair next to Clover who held a pen in her hand.

"I'm in the dining room," Parker's whisper tickled Wyatt's ear.

"I'm in the kitchen behind the island," Isaac said. "I've got a clear shot for Chris."

Wyatt slid to the right, blocking Chris. While he knew Chris had been in on the scheme, he got the feeling that Chris wasn't part of the master plan. And as much as he had no feelings of empathy for this redheaded chick and he couldn't care less about Trisha, he didn't see the need to make them all collateral damage, unless he had to.

"Okay. Guess we're not taking out Chris," Isaac said. "Repositioning myself so I can get a shot of the redhead. And not a shoot to kill shot."

"We're about to have company," Landon said. "Cops are less than five minutes out."

Time to end this charade.

"Don't sign it," Wyatt commanded.

Trisha pushed the gun into Clover's temple.

Clover gasped and dropped the pen to the floor.

"Stupid bitch," Trisha muttered. "Pick it up."

Out of the corner of Wyatt's eye, he saw a shadow slink across the kitchen floor. Julie stood on the other side of Chris, her weapon pointed at Wyatt's chest. The bloody knife still lay on the table, only inches from Clover's hand.

Clover glanced over her shoulder as she reached for the pen.

He did his best to motion toward the knife with his eyes. Hopefully, she understood. But even if she didn't, Wyatt was going to make sure if anyone took a bullet, it would be him.

"Trisha, you're forgetting one thing," Wyatt said. "And that's Keanu is alive, and he saw Chris and Julie abduct Clover, and I bet he too recognized Julie as your stepdaughter. That's not going to bode well for you."

Trisha's lips parted, and she hesitated.

"Now," Wyatt said loud and clear. Swiftly, he kicked the gun from Trisha's hand.

Bang!

Wyatt twisted his body and watched Julie drop her weapon and grab her hand.

"Motherfucker," she screamed as blood pumped from the gaping hole in her wrist. She dropped to her knees just as Isaac tackled her.

Parker rushed in and took care of Trisha.

"Clover," he said softly, lifting her into his arms. "Are you hurt?"

She shook her head wildly, but her big blue eyes stayed lock on his gaze.

The rest of the team, including Cookie and Benny, came barreling in, followed by the local police.

Needing a few moments alone, he whisked Clover into the family room and set her down on the sofa, ignoring the shouting in the other room. He brushed the hair from her face and pressed his lips against hers in a tender, loving kiss. "I'm so sorry I left you and Keanu alone. I should have known that was a ploy to get us out of the house."

"None of this is your fault," she said, tears streaking down the sides of her face. "My own mother was going to kill me for my money, the bar, and my songs." She buried her face in the palms of her hands. "My father protected me from her for years, but I had no idea she was this ruthless." She raised her head and blinked. "What does that mean for me? I mean, I am her flesh and blood."

"You are nothing like Trisha, so don't even think that for one second. Your father did protect you from her, and I only wish I had honored him and done a better job of it myself. I hate disappointing him, and right now, I know he wouldn't be very happy with me."

"I know he's looking down on you with a smile and full of pride. Thank you for protecting me."

He rested his forehead against hers and let out a long breath. "We will be spending the next few hours giving statements and all that good stuff, but I want you to know that I plan on spending what little time I have left of my week vacation wining and dining you so you'll see that I might not make the worst boyfriend ever."

She jerked her head. "Did you just reference yourself as my boyfriend?"

He nodded, smiling like a schoolboy who just got his first kiss under the bleachers. "I know I've been all over the place, but loving you scares the shit out of me."

EPILOGUE

Four Months Later

The last time Clover waited for Wyatt to return from deployment she planned on telling him she had feelings for him.

This time she had bigger news, and she wasn't sure how he was going to take it because they had only discussed it once since they started dating.

Well, not dating, since he moved in with her right before he left three weeks ago. And for the last week, she'd been going apeshit crazy, bursting at the seams, wanting to tell someone, but she couldn't.

Not until she told Wyatt.

She sat on front stoop and stared down the street. He'd texted her at ten in the evening telling her he'd returned and would head straight home after debriefing, which could take hours. She'd set up the restaurant for a big breakfast for his team since they couldn't do their usual ritual tonight. He responded to that text with a thumbs-up emoji, but she hadn't heard from him since, and it was close to two in the morning.

The rev of an engine echoed in the distance. A single headlight appeared around the corner.

She stood and smoothed down the front of her yoga pants. The garage door hummed as it opened.

Wyatt waved as he pulled into his spot. He took off his helmet and set it on the handlebars. "I was kind of hoping you'd wait up for me." Pulling her tight to his chest, he held her in a long embrace, kissing her temple. "I missed you."

"I missed you right back." She tipped her head and was rewarded with a tender, but promising kiss. "I love you," she whispered.

"I love you more," he said.

"Doubtful." Her cheeks hurt from smiling so hard. "Let's go inside."

"And upstairs to bed." He patted her bottom. She

giggled and ran toward the stairs, taking the steps two at a time.

She skidded to a stop in front of the guest room next to the master. "I need to talk to you before we go to bed."

He arched a brow. "I've been gone for almost twenty days, and you want to talk? I don't like the sound of that."

She bit down on her thumbnail.

He batted her hand away. "What's going on?"

"I think you might want to sit down for this one."

"Now you have me nervous, so whatever it is, please, just tell me," he said.

The butterflies in her stomach turned to leap frogs. Her chest tightened, and she found it difficult to take deep breaths. "Maybe it's best if I show you." With a shaky hand, she twisted the doorknob.

On the guest bed, she'd put a big teddy bear with a card.

Wyatt stepped into the room with a puzzled expression. He glanced around with his hands on his hips before staring at her. "I'm really confused, and whatever it is it can't be that bad because you haven't stopped smiling."

"Open the card."

"What card?"

"This is not going as planned," she mumbled as she breezed past him, snagging the card and shoving it at his chest.

"Okay." He held it up to the light. "To Daddy? What the hell? This isn't for me."

"For a smart man, you are being stupid." She hugged the teddy bear that sported a T-shirt that said baby on board. "Just open it."

He shrugged, pulling out the card. He took the sonogram picture and held it up to the light. "Is this what I think it is?" He moved the image closer to his face, then pushed it farther away before bringing it close again. "Whose baby is this?" He squinted. "Or should I ask who do these twins belong to?"

"You," she blurted out.

"That's funny because in order for them to be mine, they'd have to be..." He dropped the card and the sonogram. His jaw slacked open, and his eyes burst wide.

"Yes. They are mine too. We're pregnant."

"I think I need to sit down." Wyatt's butt missed the edge of the bed, and he fell to the floor. Grabbing the image, he held it up again. "We're going to have two babies at once?"

"Yes." She lowered herself and snuggled up

against him. "I know it wasn't planned, and we haven't really talked too much about it."

"I told you I was on board with having a baby." He set the image down and shifted, shoving his hand into his pocket. "That's why I bought you this. I was hoping I could make an honest woman of you before that happened." He held up a huge diamond ring.

"Holy shit." She reached out to touch it but yanked her hand away. "Is that what I think it is?"

"I love you with all my heart and soul, Clover. Will you marry me?"

"Oh, hell yes." This time she snagged the ring and glided it on her finger. Straddling him, she held out her hand, admiring the elegant ring. "I think we need to have sex right here, right now."

"I'm not going to argue with you."

"You're a smart man," she whispered. "I love you."

Thank you for taking the time to read *Protecting Clover*. I hope you enjoyed. Please feel free to leave an HONEST review.

ABOUT THE AUTHOR

Welcome to my World! I'm a USA Today Bestseller of Romantic Suspense, Contemporary Romance, and Paranormal Romance.

I first started writing while carting my kids to one hockey rink after the other, averaging 170 games per year between 3 kids in 2 countries and 5 states. My first book, IN TWO WEEKS was originally published in 2007. In 2010 I helped form a publishing company (Cool Gus Publishing) with NY Times Bestselling Author Bob Mayer where I ran the technical side of the business through 2016.

I'm currently enjoying the next phase of my life...the empty NESTER! My husband and I spend our winters in Jupiter, Florida and our summers in Rochester, NY. We have three amazing children who have all gone off to carve out their places in the world, while I continue to craft stories that I hope will make you readers feel good and put a smile on your face.

Sign up for my Newsletter (https://dl.bookfunnel.com/6atcf7g1be) where I often give away free books before publication.

Join my private Facebook group (https://www.facebook.com/groups/191706547909047/) where I post exclusive excerpts and discuss all things murder and love!

Never miss a new release. Follow me on Amazon:amazon.com/author/jentalty

And on Bookbub: bookbub.com/authors/jen-talty

amazon.com/author/jentalty

bookbub.com/authors/jen-talty

ALSO BY JEN TALTY

Brand New Series!

It's all in the Whiskey

JOHNNIE WALKER

GEORGIA MOON

NY State Trooper Series

IN TWO WEEKS

DARK WATER

DEADLY SECRETS

MURDER IN PARADISE BAY

TO PROTECT HIS OWN

DEADLY SEDUCTION

WHEN A STRANGER CALLS

NY State Trooper Novella

HIS DEADLY PAST

Brand New Novella for the First Responders series

A spin off from the NY State Troopers series

PLAYING WITH FIRE

PRIVATE CONVERSATION

The Men of Thief Lake

REKINDLED

DESTINY'S DREAM

Other novels

JANE DOE'S RETURN

THE BUTTERFLY MURDERS

The Aegis Network

THE LIGHTHOUSE

HER LAST HOPE

THE LAST FLIGHT

THE RETURN HOME

Coming soon!

THE MATRIARCH

The Collective Order

THE LOST SISTER

THE LOST SOLDIER

THE LOST SOUL

Coming soon!

THE LOST CONNECTION

Special Forces Operation Alpha

BURNING DESIRE

BURNING KISS

BURNING SKIES

BURNING LIES

BURNING HEART

BURNING BED

REMEMBER ME ALWAYS

PROTECTING AINSLEY

The Brotherhood Protectors

ROUGH JUSTICE

ROUGH AROUND THE EDGES

ROUGH RIDE

ROUGH EDGE

The Twilight Crossing Series

THE BLIND DATE

SPRING FLING

SUMMER'S GONE

WINTER WEDDING

Witches and Werewolves

LADY SASS

ALL THAT SASS

Coming soon!

NEON SASS

PAINTING SASS

Boxsets

LOVE CHRISTMAS, MOVIES

UNFORGETABLE PASSION

UNFORGETABLE CHARMERS

A NIGHT SHE'LL REMEMBER

SWEET AND SASSY IN THE SNOW

SWEET AND SASSY PRINCE CHARMING

FINDERS KEEPERS: THE PURSE

PROTECT AND DESIRE

SWEET AND SASSY BABY LOVE

CHRISTMAS AT MISTLETOE LODGE

THE PLAYERS: OVERCOMING THE ODDS

Nove*llas*

NIGHTSHADE

A CHRISTMAS GETAWAY

TAKING A RISK

WHISPERS

There are many more books in this fan fiction world than listed here, for an up-to-date list go to www.AcesPress.com

You can also visit our Amazon page at: http://www.amazon.com/author/operationalpha

Special Forces: Operation Alpha World

Christie Adams: Charity's Heart
Denise Agnew: Dangerous to Hold
Shauna Allen: Awakening Aubrey
Brynne Asher: Blackburn
Linzi Baxter: Unlocking Dreams
Jennifer Becker: Hiding Catherine
Alice Bello: Shadowing Milly
Heather Blair: Rescue Me
Anna Blakely: Rescuing Gracelynn
Amy Briggs: Saving Sarah
Julia Bright: Saving Lorelei
Victoria Bright: Surviving Savage
Cara Carnes: Protecting Mari
Kendra Mei Chailyn: Beast
Melissa Kay Clarke: Rescuing Annabeth
Samantha A. Cole: Handling Haven
Sue Coletta: Hacked
Melissa Combs: Gallant

Anne Conley: Redemption for Misty
KaLyn Cooper: Rescuing Melina
Liz Crowe: Marking Mariah
Sarah Curtis: Securing the Odds
Jordan Dane: Redemption for Avery
Tarina Deaton: Found in the Lost
KL Donn: Unraveling Love
Riley Edwards: Protecting Olivia
PJ Fiala: Defending Sophie
Nicole Flockton: Protecting Maria
Michele Gwynn: Rescuing Emma
Casey Hagen: Shielding Nebraska
EM Hayes: Gambling for Ashleigh
Desiree Holt: Protecting Maddie
Kathy Ivan: Saving Sarah
Jesse Jacobson: Protecting Honor
Silver James: Rescue Moon
Becca Jameson: Saving Sofia
Kate Kinsley: Protecting Ava
Heather Long: Securing Arizona
Gennita Low: No Protection
Kirsten Lynn: Joining Forces for Jesse
Margaret Madigan: Bang for the Buck
Kimberly McGath: The Predecessor
Rachel McNeely: The SEAL's Surprise Baby
KD Michaels: Saving Laura

Wren Michaels: The Fox & The Hound
Kat Mizera: Protecting Bobbi
Mary B Moore: Force Protection
LeTeisha Newton: Protecting Butterfly
Angela Nicole: Protecting the Donna
MJ Nightingale: Protecting Beauty
Sarah O'Rourke: Saving Liberty
Victoria Paige: Reclaiming Izabel
Anne L. Parks: Mason
Debra Parmley: Protecting Pippa
Lainey Reese: Protecting New York
TL Reeve and Michele Ryan: Extracting Mateo
Elena M. Reyes: Keeping Ava
Angela Rush: Charlotte
Rose Smith: Saving Satin
Jenika Snow: Protecting Lily
Lynn St. James: SEAL's Spitfire
Dee Stewart: Conner
Harley Stone: Rescuing Mercy
Jen Talty: Burning Desire
Megan Vernon: Protecting Us

Police and Fire: Operation Alpha World

Freya Barker: Burning for Autumn
KaLyn Cooper: Justice for Gwen
Aspen Drake: Sheltering Emma

Deanndra Hall: Shelter for Sharla

Barb Han: Kace

CM Steele: Guarding Hope

Reina Torres: Justice for Sloane

Stacey Wilk: Stage Fright

As you know, this book included at least one character from Susan Stoker's books. To check out more, see below.

SEAL of Protection: Legacy Series

Securing Caite
Securing Brenae (novella)
Securing Sidney
Securing Piper
Securing Zoey (Jan 2020)
Securing Avery (May 2020)
Securing Kalee (Sept 2020)

Delta Team Two Series

Shielding Gillian (Apr 2020)
Shielding Kinley (Aug 2020)
Shielding Aspen (Oct 2020)
Shielding Riley (TBA)
Shielding Devyn (TBA)
Shielding Ember (TBA)
Shielding Sierra (TBA)

Delta Force Heroes Series

Rescuing Rayne (FREE!)

Rescuing Aimee (novella)

Rescuing Emily

Rescuing Harley

Marrying Emily (novella)

Rescuing Kassie

Rescuing Bryn

Rescuing Casey

Rescuing Sadie (novella)

Rescuing Wendy

Rescuing Mary

Rescuing Macie (Novella)

Badge of Honor: Texas Heroes Series

Justice for Mackenzie (FREE!)

Justice for Mickie

Justice for Corrie

Justice for Laine (novella)

Shelter for Elizabeth

Justice for Boone

Shelter for Adeline

Shelter for Sophie

Justice for Erin

Justice for Milena

Shelter for Blythe

Justice for Hope

Shelter for Quinn

Shelter for Koren
Shelter for Penelope

SEAL of Protection Series

Protecting Caroline (FREE!)
Protecting Alabama
Protecting Fiona
Marrying Caroline (novella)
Protecting Summer
Protecting Cheyenne
Protecting Jessyka
Protecting Julie (novella)
Protecting Melody
Protecting the Future
Protecting Kiera (novella)
Protecting Alabama's Kids (novella)
Protecting Dakota

New York Times, USA Today and *Wall Street Journal* Bestselling Author Susan Stoker has a heart as big as the state of Tennessee where she lives, but this all American girl has also spent the last fourteen years living in Missouri, California, Colorado, Indiana, and Texas. She's married to a retired Army man who now gets to follow *her* around the country.

www.stokeraces.com
www.AcesPress.com
susan@stokeraces.com

Made in the USA
Monee, IL
13 January 2020

20277447R00095